The Visitor Series

The Visitor Makes a Retreat

The Visitor Meets Old Hairy

The Visitor Sees a Ghost

The Visitor Plays a Game

The Visitor Kids Around

The Visitor Has a Ball

The Visitor Catches a Bouquet

The Visitor

Plays a Game

Book 4 by Shawna Robison Young

Write Integrity Press

Dedication

For my family
who has supported me
in this writing journey.
Remember to go after your dreams
and don't give up on the impossible

because . . .

"Impossible is a dare." -Muhammad Ali

Contents

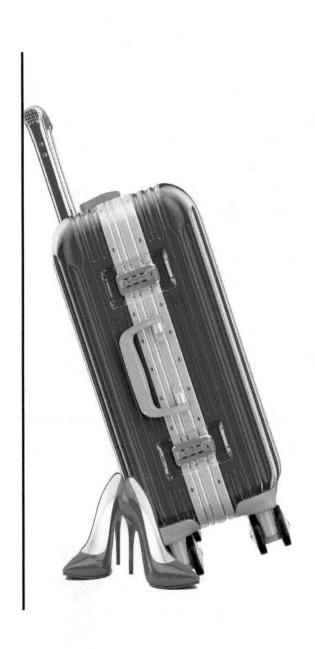

Chapter One

Knocked it out of the Park

Teagan Wright pulled it off and with five minutes to spare. She sat the last balloon in place on the large arch that spanned the stage. She scanned the gym. Its transformation into a ballroom had taken all day and still there were a few workers, like her, scurrying through the many tables and chairs. She let out a long sigh as she held her golden brown hair upward off her clammy neck.

Bistro lights dangled from each corner of the room. They met in the middle above a three-string pendant chandelier. The thirty round tables covered in white cloths occupied the middle of the space. Each one was topped with circle-mirror centerpieces and glass vases holding tall, white Calla Lilies.

Rectangle tables, along the sides of the room, held forty-five silent auction baskets. That had been her part of the process. And up here on the stage more than thirty items for live bid waited. Decorating and setting up these areas had been her part of the program, and it looked pretty good, even to her. She trotted down the steps to the food preparation section of the ballroom.

A multi-layer white cake embossed with intricate detail, handmade sugar flowers, candy pearls and crystals occupied the table in the middle of the room. The baker took several one-layer cakes with the same design from a cart and placed them around the main one.

Teagan made her way toward the cake. "That looks delicious and so beautiful, Betty."

"Why thank you, dear." The heavy-set forty-something woman's high-pitched voice sounded childlike. "Don't get so busy tonight that you forget to get a slice."

"I won't. It would be a sin to not try one of your heavenly creations." Teagan nodded.

Betty giggled at Teagan's use of the baker's slogan. "That it would be. But seriously, be sure to not only eat the cake, but the meal too." She sniffed the air. "Talk about heavenly. Doesn't it smell amazing? I took a peek back in the kitchen. Chicken marsala. Have you been to Chef Marco's Italian Bistro yet?

"I have." Teagan had gone with Dad for the grand opening a few months back. It's the reason she'd suggested Marco cater the fundraiser.

Betty put her thumb and forefingers together, kissed them, and separated them into the air. "It's magnifico."

"It sure is."

"Now, I mean it. You take care of yourself and eat tonight. In fact, I'm going to save you a slice of cake just to be sure you get one. What flavor would you like?"

"Red velvet?"

"Ah, yes. Red velvet is my specialty."

"Aren't they all?"

Betty laughed. "Touché. I can't deny that." She touched Teagan's jawlines with both of her hands. "Oh, sweetie. Are you wearing your mom's earrings?"

Teagan nodded.

"They look stunning on you. You know she'd be so proud of you."

Teagan again nodded and blinked away the tear threatening to fall.

Betty wiped at her own tears sitting on the edge of her eyes, and then she kissed Teagan's cheek. "You look beautiful tonight."

"Thank you."

Betty looked behind her and then back at Teagan. "I better go get the display cake for the live bid out of the van and put on the final touches."

The change of subject by Betty had been on purpose, no doubt.

Betty turned and dashed out of the room.

Someone touched Teagan's shoulders, and he whispered in her ear. "Everything looks great."

She turned and smiled at her best friend. "Doesn't it though?" Everyone had worked so hard, but Teagan had the extra pressure of wanting to impress Aunt Connie.

Ty shook his head. "Girl, it's on point. Especially the fancy duds over there." He looked toward the stage where she'd been working. "This place is dope. Like a pro did it." His gaze fell upon her. "And whoa, you look stunning." He held her hand with his soft brown one and spun her around.

"Thanks." She looked down at her wine-colored jumpsuit embroidered with gold-floral, antique lace. Definitely not her normal everyday tee shirt and jeans attire. Her glasses slid to the brim of her nose, and she pushed them back into place. "I think everything came together well."

"Your Aunt . . . what did you say her name is?"

"Aunt Connie."

"Yes, your Aunt Connie is gonna be impressed. Not only is the venue great but look at all the items you have up for bid." He tucked his fingers around the collar of his walnut-brown pinstriped suit jacket and spun around on his heel. "I mean, come on. You've got the best item up for bid right here. You know all the ladies will be biddin' top dolla'."

Teagan grinned and shook her head. He did look sharp in his suit, yellow dress shirt, and red tie. "More likely some parent is going to pay big bucks for their son or daughter to hang out with you, the YouTube star. This fundraiser is not let's-find-a-date-for-Ty."

"Why not?" He popped his collar.

She shook her head. "You are too much. You know it."

He shrugged his shoulders and raised an eyebrow. "In all seriousness, either way, I do hope I can bring in a little money for The Young Athletes Scholar Organization. I'd be nothing without them. I'm happy to do what I can. Let me know what you need tonight."

"I know Mrs. Dodger appreciates that. Once Aunt Connie arrives in a few minutes, she'll take over the event. I hope to become her right-hand woman."

A female spoke from behind Teagan. "And a fine one, I'm sure you'll be."

Recognizing the voice, Teagan turned and threw her arms around her aunt. Aunt Connie returned the hug and then smoothed down her red blouse and black dress pants. Teagan took a quick glance at her aunt's high heels. Red and stylish, of course.

Aunt Connie surveyed the room. "Wow. This is beautiful. I don't know if I could have done a better job myself. Simple yet elegant. I love the Calla Lilies and the lights. Oh wow, that cake is exquisite."

Betty had wasted no time. The beginning layers of her model cake were already up on the small round table at the edge of the arch.

Teagan fought back a squeal. That would be totally unprofessional. She needed to impress her aunt. Prove to her she could help run the foundation someday, and acting like a giddy schoolgirl would not help her case.

"We kept costs below the budget like you wanted. The more we have left over, the more we can give the charity. The baker and caterer even donated their time and food. Mrs. Dodger has all the details of that."

"Wonderful." Aunt Connie looked at Ty standing next to Teagan. "And who is this fine gentleman?"

He held his hand out. "Hello, I'm Teagan's friend, Ty."

Teagan placed her hand on his chest. "Ty is who I was telling you about. He's one of the top players on our high school basketball team, and he's recently become famous on his YouTube channel for teaching kids how to do trick shots."

Aunt Connie snapped her fingers and pointed at him. "Ah yes, and you've received a full ride to Indiana University on a basketball scholarship."

"No, ma'am, an academic scholarship, but I will be playing for the team also. Coach says I might even start. It's not normal for a player on an academic scholarship to start their freshman year, but he says if I didn't earn the academic scholarship, he was ready to give me an athletic one."

"Impressive." Aunt Connie nodded. "So can you teach me how to slam dunk?"

Ty raised his eyebrows. "Sure thing."

"A trick slam dunk?" Aunt Connie winked. "Like one of those staged basketball teams? I love going to watch them anytime they're in town."

"You bet. How about tonight after the fundraiser?"

"Fantastic."

He pointed at Aunt Connie. "You know the Brooklyn Bouncers are going to be here tonight, right?"

"Shh." Teagan put a finger over her lips. "It was a surprise."

"Oh, sorry." He grimaced.

Aunt Connie put her hands over her ears. "What? What did you say?" A smile spread across her face from ear to ear. "I didn't hear anything." She winked.

"Sure, you didn't." Teagan cocked her head sideways.

Aunt Connie held up her hand and separated her four fingers into a V. "Scout's honor."

"That's the Star Trek Vulcan salute not the Boy Scout's." Teagan laughed.

"Oh yeah." Aunt Connie chuckled. "Either way, I promise I'll be surprised."

Whispering, Ty covered the side of his mouth as if he was trying to conceal his conversation with Aunt Connie from Teagan, but Teagan heard every word. "Maybe I can get a few of them to join us for your slam dunk master class."

Aunt Connie mouthed, "That would be amazing."

"Pssst." Ryan Dodger, the cutest guy known to women, whispered from the stage. "Pssst, Ty. Hey, Ty, come here." Ryan's strawberry blond hair lay swooped across his right eyebrow. He whipped his head backward moving his hair away from his piercing blue eyes.

Ty motioned with his head toward his friend. "Speaking of basketball scholarship, my man, right here, Ryan did receive a full ride to play ball at IU. He's our point guard." He looked at him. "What's up, dude?"

"We need to talk." Ryan motioned backstage with his head. "It's . . . important."

"All right. I'll be right there. Let me see if these ladies need anything first."

Ryan raised a hand as he walked forward to the auction table. "Hey, Teagan."

Teagan's stomach fluttered. She'd known Ryan her whole life. It'd only been in the last six months that she'd started seeing him as something more than her friend. "Hey."

Ryan ran his hand along the table in front of him and then put his hands in his pockets. "You look nice."

Heat rose to her cheeks. "Thank you. You, too."

Why did she say that? Of course, he looked good, but he was wearing workout pants and a black t-shirt. He clearly still had to get ready for the event.

"Thanks. Is this your Aunt Connie that my

mom told me about?"

Aunt Connie took a step toward the stage and held her hand out. "I'm the one and only."

Ryan looked at her hand and then quickly at the table and back up as he made his way to the end of the stage. He took Aunt Connie's hand. "Nice to meet you."

"Likewise. And who is your mother?"

"Amy Dodger," Teagan announced for him. "Her brother started The Young Athletes Scholar Organization twenty-five years ago. Mrs. Dodger took it over after he passed away last year."

"Ah, yes."

"Mom wanted me to let you know she'll be here soon." Ryan glanced at Ty with widened eyes. "She got caught up . . . uh . . . with something." He pulled out his phone from his pocket and looked down at it. "I'm sorry to take Ty from you ladies, but I need to talk to him really quick. I'll have him right back to you."

"Not a problem. Take your time," Aunt Connie said.

With what looked like little effort, Ty hopped on to the stage with a box jump motion next to Ryan.

Teagan playfully rolled her eyes. "Show off."

Ty spun around on his heels. "Like I said, your best item up for bid."

"Ha. Ha." Teagan shook her head. "Get out of here."

Ty clicked his tongue, shot a finger gun in her direction, and then followed Ryan backstage.

"Hurry up." Ryan said, his voice agitated as it carried from behind the stage curtains. "I need you right now. We have to take care of the situation."

"I'm coming, dude. Chill."

"It's bad. Come on."

"You guys, okay?" What was bad? What was going on? "Can I help out?"

The backstage door screeched as it opened and then slammed shut.

Chapter Two

One Bad Move Doesn't Define the Player

Teagan wrung her fingers. She hoped Ryan was okay. It wasn't like him to be so agitated, but the last several weeks, he'd been out of sorts and on edge. She'd have to ask Ty later what was going on with Ryan. For now, she needed to focus back on the gala.

She turned to her aunt. "So, what do you want me to do? How can I help?"

"It looks like everything's done. I'm guessing we just have a few last-minute details to line up, so in the meantime, show me around. What items do we have up for bid?"

Teagan took Aunt Connie through the room

showing each basket in the silent auction, the suggested bid amount, and who contributed the items.

"These are amazing. I might just bid on this one myself." Aunt Connie lifted a woman's pampering basket and tilted it around for a better look at the items inside: a white bathrobe, matching slippers, a set of body wash, body mist, and lotion, a candle, tall bottle of bubble bath, a mystery book, box of chocolates, and more.

"Mrs. Dodger donated this one. Actually, she contributed several of the baskets and many items for the live auction. She also had one of her travel agent friends donate a ten-day cruise to the Caribbean Islands. Mrs. Dodger is one of the nicest people I've ever met. Her brother was too. People would do anything for them."

"What a blessing to have her continue her brother's legacy by taking over the organization. Family run businesses are the best."

Of course, her aunt would feel that way. But Teagan wholeheartedly agreed. "Speaking of family run businesses, I'd love to talk with you about my future working for the foundation after college. Did

Dad tell you I've been accepted to the University of Chicago."

"He did. Go Maroons! Congratulations." Aunt Connie touched the side of Teagan's arm. "I'm so proud of you. As far as you being a part of the foundation someday, of course, that can happen."

Teagan squelched a squeal again.

Aunt Connie's eyebrows furrowed. "I just want you to be sure it is what you want out of life. It can be stressful and takes a lot of organizational skills, which you've proven you have. There is little room for error. Perfection is the key to success. This life is hectic and busy, sleeping in hotel rooms a lot, or crashing at friends and families' homes. And even though my parents did it, and your dad and I traveled everywhere with them, it's not conducive for family life. We were so rarely at home that it didn't really feel any different from the hotels. Don't get me wrong, I loved every minute of it as a kid and now, but it's not for everyone. Your dad being one of them."

"Yes, Dad's told me it can be lonely."

"It can be, but so rewarding too. When the time comes for you to decide about your future and the foundation, pray on it and see where the Lord leads."

"I will."

"Good. All right now, show me the items up for live auction."

Aunt Connie followed Teagan up the steps to the stage. The tables were filled with high-end items, all-inclusive trips, time with top-athletes and coaches, season tickets to ball games and Broadway shows, plus more.

Betty stood in front of her masterpiece and piped some repairs on one of her cake layers.

"Oh, wow. Is this cake up for bid?" Aunt Connie asked.

"Yes, and it includes a booking for anytime within this year or next to have my bakery create a cake for an event."

Teagan chimed in. "Betty's cakes are the most sought out in the area. The waiting list to book her for an event is normally close to two years."

Betty laughed. "She exaggerates. It doesn't always take that long, but I do stay booked most of the year."

"What a great item for auction." Aunt Connie licked her lips. "I look forward to trying a piece of cake later."

"Thank you. I hope you enjoy it."

"She will." Of course, it would be a piece of the real cake. Not this boxed model.

Betty stepped backward and eyed her creation for a moment with her head tilted. Then with a nod, she turned toward Teagan. "I forgot the topper in the van. I'll be right back." She hurried backstage where the loading doors were.

Aunt Connie put a hand on Teagan's shoulder. "You and the other volunteers have done a fantastic job. I'm truly impressed. These items will surely bring in lots of money."

Teagan hoped so. She wanted to make it possible to provide a plethora of programs for underprivileged kids through The Young Athlete Scholar Organization. Maybe even help Mrs. Dodger branch out YASO to other communities outside of Floyds Knobs, Indiana.

Teagan couldn't contain the words. "How amazing would it be if we raised enough for more boys and girls to learn from college and pro coaches and star athletes. Can you imagine how special that is for kids whose parents can barely afford tennis shoes to now be blessed with baseball equipment, gymnastic leotards, and skills camps run by athletes and coaches at the top of their games at no cost? You know what else is amazing about this organization?"

"What?"

"They don't just focus on the athletic skills of a kid, but also on their academics. Ty was six when he started at YASO. He was a struggling first grader. He couldn't read or spell or count past thirty. YASO got him tutors and built his confidence. Now look at him, going to IU on a full-ride academic scholarship. That is why I want to work for the foundation. There are so many organizations we can assist, so many lives and communities we can help change, and men and women we can support who have dreams of creating their own foundations."

"You have the bug, that's for sure!"

"I want to do good." Teagan glanced down at the table.

Something didn't look right. Was something missing? She surveyed the table. She ran through the list in her head. The Hawaii trip-check. Day with Ty: the YouTube channel star-check. Day with quarterback Terry Timber from the Louisville

Legend pro team-check. College basketball tournament tickets-check. World Soccer tournament tickets-check. Private gymnastics instruction by gold-medalist Gwendolyn Driver-check.

"Everything okay?" Aunt Connie asked.

Teagan nodded. She couldn't tell her aunt she'd possibly forgotten something. Perfection was key.

Teagan ran through the rest of the items in her mind, eyeing the auction list on the clipboard laying on the table. All there. What was missing? It appeared nothing.

She drew in a deep breath and looked up. Relax.

Across the room, Ryan's mother stood in the doorway and stared in Teagan's direction.

Teagan waved to her as she spoke to Aunt Connie. "That's Mrs. Dodger."

Without acknowledging Teagan or her aunt, Mrs. Dodger looked down at her phone, raked her hand across the top of her head, and then rubbed her temples. She exhaled and then turned and walked out of the room.

"I'll introduce you to Mrs. Dodger in a little bit. Ryan says she stays busy."

"And she runs this organization well. What a saint."

"She is. Such a generous person, too." Teagan lifted her hand to the auction table.

That was it—what was missing. The voucher that Mrs. Dodger's friend had donated. The one for the ten-day cruise to the Caribbean Islands. Where was it? Teagan had brought it with everything else. It had to be here.

Mrs. Dodger had handed it to her personally yesterday. Teagan had put it in her backpack inside her binder with all the other vouchers and certificates. She'd counted all of them today, before she placed them on the table.

Hadn't she double, triple checked? How had she overlooked it?

A little fender bender with a stop sign this morning had frazzled her for like two minutes, but then she'd gotten over it and had gotten right down to business. Where could it be?

Think.

She'd gotten home last night and put her backpack on a chair at the breakfast bar. Ty and Ryan had come over to help her organize the auction list. Ty got into her backpack to get out her Chromebook. Ryan got in the refrigerator for orange juice. Dad called for her to come to his office down the hallway to tell him hi. When she'd returned, the guys were sitting at the table with hoagie sandwiches and a bag of chips in front of them. She'd laughed and told them to help themselves. They always did. She'd pulled the binder out of her backpack. Ty typed the items on the list document while she read them and then checked them off with her green glitter pen.

She'd had Ty put the Caribbean Islands Cruise on the list. She was sure of it.

Ryan had even pulled the voucher out of her hand and read over it. "I want to go on this cruise."

Ty held up his hand for a high five. "Graduation trip!"

Ryan left him hanging, so Teagan gave Ty a high-five instead. "And how are we going to pay for that?"

Ryan tossed the voucher at Ty. "Maybe if you

actually made money from your YouTube channel like every other YouTube star, then you could bid on the cruise. Or maybe even help a friend in need."

Ty picked up the voucher and threw it back. "Maybe you should tell mommy you want to go, and she can just buy you a trip. You guys are loaded."

"You know she can't." Ryan clenched his jaws.

Even mad he'd looked incredibly cute. Why had he been so tense, though?

Teagan had grabbed the voucher. "Hey now, stop throwing this around. It's worth over $10,000."

Ryan had pushed hard against the table and slid his chair backward, moving the table forward. He'd stormed down the hallway toward the bathroom, and Ty followed. Teagan had remained at the table straining to eavesdrop, but she could only hear mumbles.

A few minutes later, they'd returned, smiling, and laughing like the best of friends.

What had Teagan done with the voucher after she'd taken it from the boys? Surely, she'd put it back in the binder. It wasn't like her to not put something back where it belonged. But what if she hadn't? Maybe it was lying on the kitchen table. Did she have time to run home and look?

The door from backstage slammed shut, and Ty stormed in, grumbling under his breath.

"What's wrong?" Teagan asked.

Ty glanced past her toward her Aunt Connie. "Nothing. I'm fine."

Aunt Connie probably noticed his mood change. It was obvious. She touched Teagan's arm. "I'm going to go find Mrs. Dodger to introduce myself and finish getting things set for tonight." She leaned toward Teagan's ear. "Talk with your friend, and when you're done, come find me."

Aunt Connie left the room.

"What's up?" Teagan asked.

Ty hit his fist into his palm. "It's nothing. I'll deal with it. Don't worry about it."

"But I am worried. What's wrong? Is Ryan okay?"

Ty blew out a breath and scanned the room as if searching for something. "I hope so. Everything's a mess."

"What's a mess?"

"Truly, we have everything handled. You have this gala to worry about. Can I do anything to help?

I can take care of the other situation later."

"Are you sure everything is fine?"

"Yep. What can I do?"

She didn't believe him, but she could use his help. "Can you run by my house and see if I left the cruise voucher there? Maybe on the kitchen table. I can't find it. I swore it was here."

"Ah shoot. Yeah, I'll go look. Is your dad home?"

"No, he should be on his way here. You remember where we hide the key, right?"

"Yeah."

"Please keep this quiet. I don't want Aunt Connie to find out I screwed up."

"No problem." Ty rushed backstage, and the door slammed shut announcing his exit.

Wait. Teagan remembered the hideaway key was missing yesterday. Nothing too alarming. From time to time, her police officer dad would use it and leave it in his pocket. He didn't like having the hideaway key, anyway. He always said it invites in burglars.

She grabbed her purse and ran toward the back door in hopes of giving Ty her house key before he left. She flung the door open as Ryan rushed in and knocked her flat on her back onto the floor. He hovered over her, staring at her. Her heart pounded hard, feeling like a heroine in a romance novel.

Without a word or helping her up, he ran off. She stuck her bottom lip out in a playful pout, stood, and continued on her mission to get Ty the key. She opened the backstage door.

Ty stood next to his jeep and toe to toe with a short brunette female wearing designer jeans and a cream-colored top. Teagan huffed. Even though she couldn't see the girl's face, Teagan could recognize her arch nemesis anywhere. Why would Ty date such a mean-girl like Lacey Brown?

Ty shook his head and spoke intently. Lacey reached for him, but he jerked away. He pulled his keys from his pocket, turned, unlocked his car, and got inside. He shut the door, and she slammed her hands against the driver's side window.

Teagan's stomach dropped. Why did he put up with Lacey? He deserved someone so much better.

Ty backed up his car and pulled out of the parking lot.

"Come back. Please!" Lacey shouted.

Teagan took a step forward to tell Lacey to go home, but a blood-curdling scream came from somewhere inside the building, and Lacey darted toward the woods next to the parking lot.

Chapter Three

Down for the Count

The shrill cry from the woman inside the YASO building echoed in Teagan's ear. Forget chasing Lacey into the woods to confront her. Teagan ran through the door and the empty backstage area, she jumped from the stage, and ran out of the ballroom into the front hallway. There, she stopped and surveyed her surroundings, looking and listening for further signs of where the scream had come from. What sounded like laughter came from down the hallway. Well, that was weird. She followed the sound toward the small office.

Inside Mrs. Dodger's office, Aunt Connie stood leaning slightly forward with one hand on her hip and the other covering her laughing mouth. Mrs.

Dodger sat behind her desk with her face buried in one hand and the other placed on top of her desk.

Teagan gasped. "What is going on? Did you all hear that scream?"

Mrs. Dodger wiped the tears from her face. "Oh dear. I'm so sorry. Your aunt walked in to introduce herself and startled me. My back was turned, and I just happened to be thinking about the garter snake that's hiding in the landscaping out front. It slithered in front of me earlier today." She shuddered and then laughed. "So silly now, but for a brief second, I swore Connie's knocking on my door was the snake's tail smacking against the door and her 'hello' was him hissing at me."

Aunt Connie held her hand out to Mrs. Dodger. "It'sssss nicccce to meet you."

Mrs. Dodger took her hand, and the two women chuckled again.

Teagan smiled. "I'm glad to see you ladies are okay."

"Yes, all good. Just a little embarrassed," Mrs. Dodger tapped her heart. "Have you seen Ryan? He said he'd be here."

"I did see him a few minutes ago. He wasn't

dressed for the event yet and seemed to be in a hurry."

Mrs. Dodger picked up a pair of scissors from her desk. She waved them as she spoke. "Oh, that boy. Always on the go and always late." She stood, grabbed a piece of paper, and held it to her chest. "I better go check on him. See you ladies in the ballroom shortly. I think this is going to be the most memorable gala yet. Great job, Teagan."

Teagan looked at Aunt Connie. "Since I know everyone is okay, I also need to check on something. I will be right back."

Teagan hurried back outside. There was no sign of the girl who had disappeared into the woods. The parking lot held only a few cars: Mrs. Dodger's silver van, Teagan's blue Camry, Betty's blue van, Marco's sporty red car, and an old vintage looking yellow Mustang with Kentucky tags, most likely her aunt's rental. Soon the parking lot would be full of vehicles.

She pulled out her phone from her pocket and dialed Ty's number. It went straight to voicemail.

Ah. Ty always forgot to charge his cell. "Ty, it's Teagan. I'm hoping your phone isn't dead, and you'll get my message. Call me as soon as you get this?"

She hung up, texted the same message, and then checked the time: six fifteen. People would start arriving anytime now for the seven o'clock event. Taking in a deep breath, she settled her nerves. Ty should have arrived at her house by now. Hopefully, Dad had returned the key to its hidden location, Ty found the cruise voucher, and was on his way back already. Then she would sneak it onto the table as if it had always been there. No one would know the difference.

Dad pulled his police cruiser into the parking lot, flashed his siren lights at her, and honked the horn. She waved. He stepped out of the vehicle. "Hey, darling. Aunt Connie arrive yet?"

"Yes, sir. She's inside."

He hugged her. "You look beautiful." He looked down at his uniform. "I've got my suit in the back of cruiser. I'm going to run on in and get ready."

"Hey, big brother," Aunt Connie said from behind them.

Aunt Connie took off her heels, ran to him, and

put her arms around him. "It's been too long."

He picked her up from the ground and swung her around. "Hey, little sis."

Aunt Connie swatted at her brother's arm. "Put me down, Paul."

He obliged. "But you're so little and fun sized." He patted the top of her head as his six-feet-four-inch frame towered a foot over her.

Aunt Connie punched his arm. "But I'm mighty."

He rubbed his arm. "That you are." He touched Teagan's shoulder. "My girl has been working hard with this event. She's got your same work ethic, that's for sure. Working night and day. Rattling off about how much more YASO can do after this fundraiser. It's definitely felt like the Twilight Zone the last few months."

Aunt Connie cleared her throat. "And that's a good thing, right."

He made a playful smirk and shrugged his shoulders. "No, seriously. I've loved seeing her passion for the foundation. It does bring back some wonderful memories."

Aunt Connie nodded. "That it does. Teagan and

I'd better get in there before the guests arrive. How about a game of Clue later tonight if it's not too late?"

Teagan's ears perked. "Clue? It's never too late for a game of Clue." Her favorite.

He laughed. "You two always give me a run for my money with that game. Yes, let's play tonight even though Connie's going to win like always."

Aunt Connie tucked her arm into Teagan's and led the way back toward the building. From the corner of her eye, Teagan caught a glimpse of Mrs. Dodger struggling as she carried a laundry basket with blankets and pillows and a large tote bag along her forearm toward the side of the building.

She hesitated and pulled away from her aunt, moving toward the other woman. "You need help?" Teagan called out.

Mrs. Dodger looked in her direction, popped the basket upward into her arms, and rushed around the back of building.

"I'm going to go help her." Teagan followed Mrs. Dodger down the hill to the basement door.

Fumbling with her basket on one hip and a set of keys in the opposite hand, Mrs. Dodger attempted to unlock the door.

"Can I help you?" Teagan reached for the laundry basket, but Mrs. Dodger leaped and dropped the basket, spilling all its contents.

"Oh, you startled me."

Goodness, Mrs. Dodger was jumpy today. Teagan bent down and returned the blankets and pillows into the basket. "Can I help you carry this in?"

"No, thank you. I've got it." Mrs. Dodger unlocked the door and held it open with her backside as she bent down to pick up the basket. "My washer went out at home. I thought I'd throw a load in here before the gala. A mother's work is constant."

An apple rolled out of the tote bag. Teagan picked it up and dropped it into Mrs. Dodger's bag alongside more fruit and boxes of granola bars and breakfast tarts. "It looks like you're struggling with all this."

"Nah, I've got it, but thanks." Mrs. Dodger slid on in and shut the door.

The pounding of footsteps and crunching leaves came from the woods behind Teagan. She turned, and the sounds stopped. She touched her jumpsuit pocket for her pepper spray as she squinted, trying for a better look into the woods.

"Anybody there?" Teagan slid her hand into her pocket.

A deer darted out from the woods. She gasped as she pulled out her pepper spray and pointed it in the animal's direction. She laughed at herself and then returned the canister to her pocket as the deer ran into another section of the woods.

Teagan started her ascent up the hill. The sound of footsteps and crunching leaves resumed while someone from inside the woods whistled. She darted toward the front door. A chill ran down her spine. Had someone been watching her?

Where was Ty? He hadn't returned yet or called or texted. Teagan paced backstage and fidgeted with her hands. She should come clean and tell Aunt Connie about the missing voucher. She exhaled. No, Ty would be back.

She peeked out from behind the curtain. The

ballroom was filled with people sitting at the dinner tables and standing around the silent auction basket tables. The waiters and waitresses carried trays of beverages to the guests. Chef Marco, Betty, and Mrs. Dodger mingled among the people. Aunt Connie spoke with a couple of the Brooklyn Bouncers. Good for her. An Olympic gold-medal gymnast and an NFL quarterback sat among the guests, giving autographs, and posing for pictures.

Mrs. Dodger waved to the guest she'd been talking with and to other people as she made her way out of the ballroom. Claire Stein, head cheerleader at the high school, entered through the doorway passing Mrs. Dodger. Claire was sweet but was best friends with Lacey. Again, how anyone could like Lacey was beyond Teagan. Once upon a time Lacey had been a nice girl, but overnight one elementary school evening she'd changed for the worst.

Teagan's phone vibrated in her pocket. Ty! Thank goodness.

"Did you find it? Are you on the way back?"

"I didn't find it. The key was missing, and all the doors and windows were locked. I peeked through the dining room window though and didn't see the voucher. I even tried to pick the front door lock, but Colonel Mustard was barking, and your crazy neighbor was sitting on the porch watching me like a hawk. He asked what I was doing. I told him, but I don't think he believed me. He called someone on his cell and then went inside. Just in case he called the police, I got out of there. It wasn't until I was down the road that I realized my phone was dead. It just came back on. I'm about to pull into the parking lot. I'm sorry I didn't find it."

Teagan's heart sank. "It's okay. It's my fault. I should have said something to Mrs. Dodger and Aunt Connie right away. You know you really should charge your phone. It's not safe."

"I know. I know, Mom." His tone playful. "You and my actual mom have told me a thousand times. What if an axe murderer was after me and my phone was dead?"

"Or a psycho girlfriend?"

"Stop." His voice no longer playful.

"What? Lacey is crazy."

"You don't know her."

"Of course, I do. She's tormented and bullied me since fifth grade. If I could get rid of Lacey and hide the body so she couldn't fool another person into thinking she's so great, I would. I mean I watch enough crime shows, I could totally get away with it."

"You are not funny."

"I'm not trying to be. I don't like her. I don't see how you could date someone who has treated me, your best friend, so awful all these years."

"She's different now. Get to know her."

"No. Thank you." Teagan shook her head.

"I'm telling you after her mom died last year, it's changed her. You two have a lot in common now."

Teagan balled her fist. "Did you really just bring up our mothers' deaths like we should bond over these horrific tragedies? Ty, you are so clueless sometimes. You infuriate me. You and Lacey deserve each other. You are digging your own grave, you know it."

"Look, I have enough to deal with right now without your condescending comments."

Someone behind her cleared their throat. Teagan turned.

Claire pointed toward the ballroom. "Mrs.

Dodger is looking for you."

Teagan nodded. "Look Ty. I've got to go. I'll meet you in the parking lot in a minute."

His car door slammed. "Don't bother. I'll see you inside."

"Don't be like that. You know we always enter this fundraiser together."

"Not this year. You go do what you have to do. I'm going to stand out here for a minute and cool off. I'll be in a minute."

"Ty?"

"No."

"Fine. Whatever."

"What the heck?" Fear rang in his voice. "What are you doing? Stop! Stop!" He shouted.

"Ty, what's going on?"

A scuffle ensued. Was Ty running or was someone attacking him?

Teagan darted toward the door.

Umph!

The sound from her friend and the groaning that followed picked up her pace.

She ran out the back door and looked around the parking lot.

Where was he? "Ty!" she called.

Then she spied his car in the crowded lot.

She ran forward and slid to a stop.

Several yards from his vehicle, Ty lay limp on the ground covered in blood. She looked around. She found no one, only a parking lot full of empty cars. She dialed 9-1-1 before she fell by Ty's side. "Ty."

He didn't respond. His eyes remained closed, and he had a cut on his head. She checked his pulse and found a light throb in his neck. She needed to retrieve the first-aid kit and a blanket from her car. "Ty, I'll be back." She choked on her tears as she pushed herself to leave him.

The Visitor Plays a Game

Chapter Four

The Curve Ball

Red, blue, and white lights swirled around Teagan as the paramedics placed Ty's unresponsive body into the ambulance. Shaking, she sat on the ground next to Ty's jeep. A policeman covered her with a blanket and then crouched down and looked her eye to eye. "I know this is difficult, but can you tell me what you saw? What you heard?"

Teagan explained everything she could remember.

Dad stood over her, frustration taking over his face. "Whoever did this ran him over and drove away." He shook his head. "I hate to ask this, but do you know of anyone who wanted to harm Ty?"

Teagan shook her head. "I can't imagine.

Everybody loves Ty. No, the person had to have been distracted and not seen Ty until it was too late."

"I hope that's the case, but either way, the person sped away and didn't stay to be sure he was okay."

The argument Ty had with his girlfriend before he left floated to Teagan's memory. "Lacey." Teagan shouted as she looked around the crowd for her.

"What about Lacey?" her father asked.

"She was here earlier." Teagan shook her head. "But I don't see her now. She ran off into the woods after she and Ty got in an argument."

"You think Lacey did this?"

She shook her head. "No." Lacey might have been a jerk, but she wasn't crazy enough to run him over with a car.

Teagan glanced over at the bystanders hovering around the outside of the building, whispering. Mrs. Dodger stood by the front door, hand on her heart, and looked all around. Betty stood next to Mrs. Dodger. Aunt Connie opened the door, followed by Marco. Aunt Connie touched Mrs. Dodger's arm. Teagan couldn't make out what they were talking about, but no doubt, her aunt was taking care of things for the fundraiser.

Huddled together, Claire and two other cheerleader friends of Lacey's spoke with a police officer. Had the other girls seen anything? Hadn't Claire been in the wings, backstage with Teagan? And where was Lacey? Surely, she'd come back to the fundraiser to support Ty. Had his and Lacey's fight kept her away?

Tires squealed as Ryan's black truck turned into the parking lot. He pulled into a spot, slammed his door, and ran to Teagan.

"What happened?" He fell to his knees next to her.

"Ty—" Teagan unable to get out the words threw up instead.

"Where have you been?" Mrs. Dodger advanced on them.

Ryan touched Teagan's back. "Are you okay?"

She shook her head.

"What is going on?" He stood. "Oh my, gosh! Where did all this blood from?"

Teagan looked up at him. The words still wouldn't come. It was all a nightmare. It couldn't have really happened.

His mother grabbed his arm. "It's Ty. He was hit by a car."

"How? What?" Ryan stumbled forward. "Is he okay?"

Dad put his hand on Ryan's shoulder and steadied him. "Ty's alive, but unconscious."

"Is anyone riding along with us?" One of the paramedics shouted as he stood at the back of the ambulance.

Dad stood. "I'll go. His mom is working at JayC. She's a cashier there."

Another police officer stepped forward. "We'll send an officer to the store for her."

"Can I go?" Teagan wiped the hot tears burning her cheeks.

"Only one person can ride up front." The paramedic closed the back door.

Her father ran toward the ambulance. "You come up in a little bit. Help Aunt Connie and Mrs. Dodger get things settled here, and I'll take care of Ty."

How could she possibly think of the fundraiser at this point?

"I'll take her up there, Mr. Wright," Ryan wiped his hand across his mouth.

Dad got in and closed the door. The sirens wailed as the ambulance raced out of the parking lot and down the street.

Ryan took Teagan's hands and helped her to her feet.

He put his arms around her.

She fell into his arms where it felt warm and safe.

"Ty's going to be okay. He's got to be okay," he whispered.

She buried her face in his chest. "How could someone just drive off like that?"

"I don't know."

Aunt Connie touched Teagan's back. "I'm going to direct everyone back in and try to salvage the rest of the night the best we can. You and Ryan go." Aunt Connie looked at him. "Will you be okay to drive?"

"I'm good. Just worried about Ty, but I'm okay to drive."

The bystanders followed Aunt Connie back inside, but Mrs. Dodger, arms across her chest, stood taut next to her son. "Where have you been?"

"Mom, this isn't the time. I've got to go. Ty—"

"No. Where have you been? You've been acting strange all day."

He widened his eyes. "Not now."

"You aren't even dressed for the event. What were you going to do—sashay your way in here dressed in a warm-up suit?"

"My dress clothes are in the back. I was going to change when I got here."

"Again, where were you? Why are you late?"

"It's nothing. I just lost track of time. Playing ball with the boys down at Romeo court. Teagan and I have to go."

Mrs. Dodger bit her lip. "Okay. I know. This is all just so awful. Why was Ty out here in the first place?" She looked at Teagan. "Wasn't he helping you?"

It was time Teagan came clean. "I misplaced the—"

"Mom, stop with the twenty questions." Ryan scowled. "Go help Teagan's aunt with the event. We're going to the hospital."

"I do need to get back in there, but this conversation isn't over." His mother pointed a shaky finger at him. "I can't stop thinking what if that had been you." She grabbed his neck and pulled him in for a hug. "Please be careful. Text me when you get there."

"I will." He turned to walk toward his truck. "Like you actually care," he whispered under his breath.

The next morning, Teagan woke in a hospital chair. Ryan slept in the chair across from her, his fist resting on his chin. His tilted head was about to lose its balance where he rested it on his hand. She itched to move the strands of his hair falling across his forehead, but she stared at him instead.

She blinked and shook her head.

Ty . . .

Last she'd heard, he was still unconscious, had several broken bones in his legs, pelvis, arms, and face. Last night they wouldn't let her or Ryan see

The Visitor Plays a Game

him. Would they today?

"There must be some kind of misunderstanding." Her father walked into the waiting room followed by a male police officer she didn't recognize. "She had nothing to do with this. He's her best friend. Like a brother to her."

The police officer pushed past him. "That may be, but I still have to bring her in for questioning." The officer stopped in front of Teagan. "Miss Wright, I need you to come with me to the station to answer questions regarding the hit and run investigation of Tyrese Jones."

Was she hearing everything correctly? Surely, they didn't think she had anything to do with it. How could she? She was on the phone with him when he got hit. She was the one who called 9-1-1. She would never. No, they must just need to ask her further questions about what she saw and heard.

"I'm telling you. You guys got it wrong. I know my daughter. She could never do anything like that."

Ryan opened his eyes and jumped. "What's going on?"

"Are you Ryan Dodger?"

"Yes, sir."

"You and your friend, Teagan are considered people of interest in the investigation of Ty—"

Ryan laughed. "You have got to be kidding. Squeaky clean Teagan and me, class president. What a joke? You are wasting your time and energy."

Teagan swallowed hard. What did they think they had on her and Ryan? She racked her brain for anything. Nothing. "Why would we hurt our friend?"

The officer crossed his arms. "That's what we're going to find out."

Teagan leaned to get a glimpse of her father at the door to the interrogation room.

"Paul, she's eighteen." Detective Evans blocked his entrance.

"I want her to have an attorney present." Dad insisted.

"I don't have anything to hide," she called out to him. "There's nothing to worry about."

"You'll have to wait out here." Detective Evans closed the door to the interview room.

Ryan had been taken to another room forcing her to do this on her own. The room smelled moldy, and all but one florescent bulb appeared burned out. Detective Evans directed her to sit in the chair against the wall next to the desk. She'd been in this room more than a hundred times before, but this time it was different. As a kid, she'd played good cop/bad cop while she waited on Dad. In fact, Ty had been with her many of those times also. Her love for solving crimes and playing Clue had come from watching him and other investigators work.

The detective held a red plastic dish of miniature chocolate bars and candies toward her. She took a Hershey kiss, and he returned the container to the desk. "Help yourself to as many as you like. There're some Kit Kats at the bottom."

"Thank you." She unwrapped the candy and popped it in her mouth. She played with the wrapper in her hand.

He laid a device on the table. "I'm recording this interview with Teagan Wright." He glanced at Teagan. "Are you aware of the recording and agree to answer my questions?"

She nodded.

The man's mouth flattened impatiently.

"Uh, yes."

"Give your name."

She repeated it for the recording.

"You're being questioned because evidence has been found to consider you a person of interest in the hit-and-run of Tyrese Jones."

"That's crazy! Ty's my best friend. I would never hurt him."

"But didn't you?"

"What?" Her heart raced. "I would never hurt him on purpose."

Detective Evans raised his eyebrows. "So, tell me about Lacey Brown."

"What about her?"

"Apparently, you are jealous of her and Ty's relationship."

Why would he think that? "No. I'm not jealous. I don't like her. She's a bully"

"You threatened her."

Teagan scoffed. "Yeah, right."

The detective cleared his throat and glanced at

his phone screen. "So, you didn't say, 'Lacey better watch her back because I watch lots of crime shows, and I know how to hide a body.'?"

Her heart raced. She had said that in so many words. Claire must have overheard. Teagan leaned her head backward and rolled her neck side to side. "It was a joke. I didn't mean it. But either way, what does it have to do with Ty? The supposed threat was to Lacey, who is awful to Ty, and I was sick of watching her hurt him. If anyone is psycho, it's her. If you don't think the hit and run was an accident, then maybe you should question her. She was in the parking lot, yelling and slamming her hands against his Jeep windows yesterday."

"You told the officers at the scene that you hadn't seen the girl's face, right?"

"No, I didn't, but—"

"I get it. You and Lacey aren't the best of friends, but you can't accuse her without proof. I know she bullied you over the Internet a couple of years ago and tried to destroy your reputation–"

"Yeah, so? I'm a big girl. I know who I am. A couple of lies and gossip doesn't change that."

"Yes, but it had to bother you."

Teagan shook her head. She couldn't care less what Lacey or anyone else at her school thought of her. Bunch of stupid teenagers. In a couple months, she'd be out of that place, in college preparing for a future helping others. "I'm fine, really."

"I can imagine how devastated you were about it."

Teagan clamped her jaw shut for a moment, swallowing the pain that still rose when she remembered it all. "Yeah, well. She got away with it. Not even a slap on the wrist. It just showed her that she can do whatever she wants."

"She got more than a slap on the wrist. She isn't allowed to have social media or Internet access without supervision until she's twenty years old."

"Like that's being monitored." Teagan huffed. "She has more followers on Instagram than I do."

He raised an eyebrow.

She looked down. "Sure, that isn't saying much, but—"

"All I'm saying is I get it. Your best friend is dating the girl who tried to ruin your reputation. It makes sense for you to be mad at him. In fact, a witness says they heard you fighting with him about

Lacey. You told him he was digging his own grave, and you'd meet him in the parking lot. That was just minutes before he was hit."

She couldn't keep her voice from shaking. "Like I told the police officer at the scene. I heard him get hit then I ran outside. I'm the one who called 911. Having a disagreement with a friend doesn't mean I wanted to kill him."

The man eyed her. "But you hate Lacey, and Ty betrayed you by dating her. You let your anger get the best of you, didn't you? Ty's mom told us she overheard you arguing with him on the phone about Lacey." He leaned toward her with his palms planted on the table.

What was he talking about?

"His mom stood at his bedroom door and listened to the argument. She heard you say you would kill him if he ever dated Lacey. And that's what you tried to do, isn't it?"

She closed her eyes hard. None of this made sense. "Oh, my goodness. I was mad. It was an expression. I didn't mean it literally. I can't even kill a little spider when I see one. I pick it up by its legs and carry it outside to freedom. I could never run my best friend over with a car."

The man straightened and took a step away from the table before he continued. "His mom found the note you left for him. The one where you said for him to watch his back because you were coming after him."

"What note? I have no idea what you're talking about." Had she ever even written those words at all?

"His mother found it under his bed in a shoebox full of notes from you. Hundreds of notes from over the years."

"The other notes may have been from me, but that one wasn't. I didn't hit him. I swear." And she was sure she hadn't even sent him a note like that, not even to goof off.

"I've seen your Camry."

Her heart raced. He really thought she'd done this.

"The damage to your front bumper is consistent with what would be expected from hitting a person."

"Or going up on the curb and accidentally hitting a street sign. I was on the way to the venue for the fundraiser yesterday morning when a cat ran out in front of me. I swerved too much and hit the sign. Since the damage was only to my car, I left and went straight to the event to set up. I had planned to tell my dad after the fundraiser."

He stared at her without emotion. "More than one witness says they saw you getting out of your car while Ty lay injured on the ground."

She ran through the moments after she found Ty. "I was getting my first-aid kit and a blanket."

The detective shook his head. "You were going to play nurse to your victim? You hit Ty, didn't you? Then you parked the car to make it look like it had been there all day. You called 9-11 and then went to get your dad."

"No." Her mind spun like a fast-paced ride at the fair.

"You told the police on the scene that Ty went back to your house to get the voucher to the cruise, but Mrs. Dodger said it was at the auction all along."

What? It hadn't been on the table. She'd searched.

Detective Evans leaned over the table again. "You planned it all, didn't you? You sent Ty to retrieve the voucher so that when he returned, you could get your revenge."

"What? No."

"You were mad at him for going out with Lacey."

"No. I swear."

"Look, I get it. The girl did a number on you. I get that you would be ticked at Ty. Rage can get the best of us."

Terror raced from the tip of her toes, up her body, and to the roots of her hair. "I didn't do it. I swear." She stood. "And I'll prove it. You can't good cop/bad cop me into a confession. I'm innocent."

"Then why else did you send him to your house for the voucher that wasn't missing?"

"It was missing." Teagan glared at him, keeping her voice steady and maintaining her eye contact. "Ty volunteered to go look for it at my house. He didn't find it."

"Of course, he didn't because it was at the fundraiser the whole time, and you know that it was. You needed him alone, so you sent him to the parking lot at a time when you knew very few people would be there. You went out to get your revenge, but then you saw him talking to some girl you thought was Lacey. It fueled your anger even more, so you waited until he returned and then you hit him with your car."

"You have it all wrong. The voucher was missing. The last place I remember seeing it was at my house. He volunteered to get it. I was on the phone with him when he pulled into the parking lot. He got out of the car. I heard him get hit. I ran outside. I checked on him. No one else was in the parking lot, so I called 9-1-1, and I ran to my car to get a blanket and my first-aid kit. Then I went back to Ty. People must have started coming out of the building when I went to my car. I didn't notice at that point. I was talking to the 9-1-1 operator and getting supplies to tend to him. Anyone who told you different doesn't have their facts straight. And yes, I can't stand Lacey. I never wanted Ty to look in her direction, but I would not hurt him because he is dating her. If I was the type of person who would do something like that, I'd go after Lacey not Ty."

Someone knocked on the door. "Come in."

The other officer whispered in the detective's ear then left, closing the door behind him.

"Lacey Brown is missing. Where were you last night?"

Teagan felt sick. Especially after all that she'd just said. "I was in the hospital. I fell asleep in the chair beside Ryan." Surely someone would verify that she'd never left. "I don't have anything to do with her missing."

The Visitor Plays a Game

Chapter Five

She came to Play

Teagan pulled the covers to her bed down and climbed in. Colonel Mustard, her trusty German shepherd, jumped onto her bed, turned in a circle twice, and then settled down in the crook of her legs. She covered her head and held her breath. Maybe if she lay perfectly still, time would stop, and she could fix everything. But how?

Yesterday morning, her biggest concern had been that her raisin bread didn't have enough raisins. Now it felt like last year all over. Dad speechless. No one listening to her. The guilty person getting away with the crime. People assuming the worst of her.

She kicked the covers off and sat up. Colonel

Mustard lifted his head and then laid it back down. She patted his soft ears. Lying here, feeling sorry for herself wouldn't accomplish anything. She had to prove her innocence, but how?

She picked up her cell and called Ryan. He didn't answer so she texted him.

CALL ME WHEN YOU GET A CHANCE.

She went to her window, opened it, and breathed in the fresh air. She looked below from the second story at her neighbor. Mr. Lewis sat on his porch rocking in his creaking chair. The sound was worse than nails running along a chalkboard. The crazy old man sat there day and night, keeping tabs on everyone. Just screeching away.

Colonel Mustard hopped off the bed and came next to her. He stuck his head above the windowsill.

Little five-year-old Johnny from across the street lost hold of his kite and it blew into Mr. Lewis's yard. The boy looked before running across the street and then froze at the edge of the sidewalk.

"Don't you dare take one step in my yard!" the old grump yelled. "That kite's mine now. You hear. You go on. Get away from my house."

Colonel Mustard barked.

"But it's my kite," the little boy whined.

"Not anymore." Mr. Lewis trudged down the porch steps and picked up the kite. "Now go home."

Her dog continued to bark.

The boy turned and darted into the street as a car rounded the corner toward him. Teagan opened her mouth to yell, but the vehicle slammed on the brakes, and Johnny made it across. The woman inside her vehicle clutched her chest.

"Stupid, kid," Mr. Lewis yelled. Then he waved the woman on.

She wiped her hand across her mouth and drove off. An image of a black car slamming into Ty in the YASO parking lot flashed through Teagan's mind. She hadn't seen it happen, of course, but when she imagined it happening, she pictured a black sedan. She shook the thought away. Who would be after Ty? And why?

A small knock came from her bedroom door, and her dog raced to it as Aunt Connie cracked it open. "Can I come in?"

"Yes."

Aunt Connie sat on the end of Teagan's bed and patted it for her to sit down next to her. Teagan obliged, and Colonel Mustard lay at her feet.

"How are you doing?" Aunt Connie ran her hand through the top of Teagan's hair to the end like a mother would do, comforting a daughter. Dad was amazing, but sometimes a woman's touch was what she needed. Thank goodness for her aunt and women like Betty in her life.

"Not good. I don't see how the police could think I did this. Ty's mom won't let me see him. And Ryan isn't answering my calls or texts. Now Lacey is missing, and they think I have something to do with that too."

Aunt Connie twirled the bottom of Teagan's hair. "They have to look into every possible scenario. Your dad and I know you could never do anything like that and so does Ty's mom and Ryan. Everyone is in shock right now. Give them some time. They'll come around. The doctors are hopeful that Ty's going to wake up. And when he does, he can tell them what happened."

Her mind wanted to believe her aunt, but her heart couldn't.

"Will you come down for dinner? Your next-door neighbor brought over a bucket of, I think he called it, yeti spaghetti and garlic bread from Chef Marco's Italian Bistro. If it's anything like his chicken marsala, it's bound to be amazing."

"It is wonderful. I love Chef Marco's yeti spaghetti." Teagan furrowed her brows. "Which neighbor?"

"I believe your dad mentioned somebody with the last name Lewis, maybe."

Surely not crazy Mr. Lewis. "The old man from next door? I just saw him out on his porch yelling at a kid."

"No, it's a young blond boy around your age. Maybe the old man's grandson, possibly?"

Teagan shrugged. "Oh, that's weird. Sounds like Julian, Mr. Lewis's nephew that he raised. He's in college, I think. I've only seen him around a few times in the last three years since he went off to college. I never really knew him when he lived there. He kept to himself and went to some private school over in Louisville."

"He's a handsome young man. Maybe he's single. Your dad invited him to stay and eat with us."

Teagan lightly smacked Aunt Connie's arm

with the back of her hand. "I'm not interested."

"Because your heart belongs to Ryan?" Aunt Connie raised her eyebrows.

"What? No. Ryan and I are just friends." Teagan looked down as her cheeks heated. Hopefully her aunt wouldn't notice. After a moment of silence, she glanced up into Aunt Connie's wide eyes.

"You positive about that? I've seen the way you look at him." Her aunt smiled.

Was she really that obvious? "Sure, he's cute, but I just have a little crush. It's not going to go anywhere. He doesn't see me as anything more than a friend."

"Well, there's always the neighbor boy downstairs who brought us dinner."

What was with her aunt? She'd never talked with Teagan about relationship things before. Was it her aunt's attempt at trying to lighten the mood? "Truly, Aunt Connie, I'm not interested in dating anyone right now. I graduate and then I'm off to college soon. Who knows? I may be like you, a contented bachelorette my whole life."

Aunt Connie put her hand on Teagan.

"Possibly, but it's okay to find your own path. Your grandma and grandpa lived happily ever after and successfully ran the foundation together. A husband and kids aren't a part of my story. It's not that I'm against being a wife or having children. It just wasn't in God's plans for me. They may very well be a part of yours. Who knows? Maybe Ryan is meant to be more than a friend, or maybe God has some future man in store for you."

Teagan appreciated what her aunt was getting at, and it was nice to have a woman to talk to about things like this, but her heart just wasn't in it. "Right now, I can't see past Ty's hit and run. What if they can't find who really did it? What if they find no other evidence and convict me of it?"

"We won't let that happen."

"How?"

"We are going to solve this and prove your innocence." Her aunt's assurance gave her a little hope, but not enough to overcome the doubts that seemed to slice through her.

"What if we can't? And besides aren't you off to your next event in a few days."

"Don't you know, I've solved 'em quicker than

that before." Aunt Connie bumped her shoulder lightly against Teagan's.

Teagan let out a sigh. "You really think we can figure out who did this to Ty?"

"I do, but let's get some food in your body before we jump right in. Okay?"

Teagan followed her aunt downstairs to the living room, with Colonel Mustard close behind them. Dad and the young blond neighbor sat at the dining room table talking. "Teagan, do you remember Julian. He's Mr. Lewis's great nephew."

Julian stood and held out his hand to her.

Teagan took his hand. "Yes, hi." Aunt Connie was right. He was incredibly handsome. Soft blond curls on top of his head, crystal blue eyes, and a smile that had the potential to possibly calm the terrified storm raging inside her.

Colonel Mustard pushed his muzzle into Julian's other hand.

Julian patted him. "Well, hello there, buddy."

"That's amazing," Teagan said. "He's normally cautious of people at first."

"Could be I smell like yeti spaghetti." He laughed.

Colonel Mustard nuzzled his head against Julian's leg. Julian bent down and rubbed the dog's head. "Do I smell good? You want a piece of me, huh?"

Colonel Mustard put his paws on Julian's shoulders and licked his face.

"Get down boy." Teagan pulled her dog with the collar. "I'm sorry. I don't know what's gotten into him." She pointed toward Colonel Mustard's bed in the living room. "Go lie down."

Her dog lowered his head, moped his way to his bed, and laid down.

Julian pulled the chair out next to his for her. "Would you mind if I wash my hands before we eat?"

Dad motioned up the stairs. "Not at all, but I'll have to send you to the upstairs washroom. The sink in the one down here is on the fritz. I haven't had a chance to fix it. Up the steps to the right at the end of the hallway."

"Thanks. I'll be right back." Julian hurried up the steps.

"Why did you invite him to stay?" Teagan looked at Dad.

"Seems like a pretty nice fellow, bringing us over dinner and all. I thought maybe you two could strike up a friendship." Dad shrugged.

"Or something more, possibly?" Aunt Connie lifted her eyebrows up and down in a playful manner.

Dad stiffened. "Maybe I shouldn't let him stay."

Teagan shook her head. "Not to worry, Dad. I'm not . . ." Pounding on the stairs hushed her as Julian quickly returned to his chair next to Teagan.

"That was fast." Teagan noted.

"I didn't want to hold you guys up."

Her stomach flip-flopped. "Thank you for bringing dinner over for us. It smells delicious."

"No problem. My uncle said your friend . . . well he didn't say it quite as nice as that . . . but he said that your friend was in a hit and run accident and is in a coma. You guys must have a lot on your minds, so I figured I'd do the neighborly thing. One less thing for you to worry about."

Aunt Connie made her way to the chair beside her brother and sat down. "How thoughtful of you, Julian."

He tipped his head slightly forward as if saying you're welcome.

"So, Julian, what's brought you to town. We don't see you much around here?" Dad asked.

"I'm taking a semester off from school. My uncle's health is declining. Cancer, so I'm here to be his caretaker, but he's rather set in his ways in case you haven't noticed." He chuckled. "I moved into those apartments at the bottom of Paoli Pike."

Dad cleared his throat. "I'm sorry. I didn't know about your uncle. He keeps to himself."

"You mean stays in his yard like a hermit and scares off any creature that dares trespass?" Julian laughed.

"Yes, that," Dad agreed.

"If you could have known him before life changed him, you would have known a completely different man. But tragedy after tragedy has made him hard."

"I get that. We've been through a lot too." Dad pointed back and forth between him and Teagan. "And being a cop, I've seen a lot too. I have to remind myself of God's goodness every day. Otherwise, I couldn't make it."

Julian nodded, but he didn't seem to understand. Then again, with an uncle like Mr. Lewis, he probably didn't have much influence from believers.

"And along that vein, why don't I go ahead and pray over our dinner." Dad clasped his hands and closed his eyes.

Teagan bowed her head but sneaked a peek at Julian. He darted a glance at Dad and then closed his eyes, his blond curls falling past his forehead, and his hands folded together on the table.

"Amen." Dad ended his prayer.

Her father picked up the spaghetti bucket and passed it to Aunt Connie. Then he did the same with the plate of garlic bread. Aunt Connie took a piece, tossed it on her plate, and then passed it on to Julian. "So what year are you in college?"

"I'm a junior."

Aunt Connie looked at Teagan. "So that would make you, how old?"

"Twenty."

"What are you studying?" Teagan took the bucket of spaghetti from Julian.

"Business Administration at UChicago."

"That's where Teagan just got accepted." The pride showed all over Dad's face.

"Congratulations. You'll love it. What are you planning to study?"

"Business."

He pointed his fork toward her. "I'd love to show you around sometime. The professors are great, and campus life is fun."

Teagan's cheeks rose with heat. "Thank you. I'd like that."

"I heard the event you planned for Young Athletes Scholar Organization raised a huge amount. Way to go. It must have been quite an evening—"

"I only planned a small part of it." Teagan's stomach dropped. She hadn't thought once of how the fundraiser had done.

Aunt Connie squeezed Teagan's hand under the table. "We did well. Thank you. And Teagan did a fantastic job getting the live auction items and everything set up. We were able to raise enough for YASO to have another successful year."

Teagan exhaled slowly. "I'm so glad. I'm sorry I didn't tell you or Mrs. Dodger about the voucher."

"Don't you worry yourself one minute about that. Besides it was there, after all. You must have overlooked it."

"But still I should have told you right away. I just didn't want to disappoint you. You always tell me perfection is key, and I thought I could handle it."

"You most certainly did not disappoint me. No one is perfect. Don't you tell anyone, but even I'm not perfect." Aunt Connie winked.

"It's crazy, all that happened last night." Julian piped in. "I heard there's a girl missing as well."

Dad raised an eyebrow at Julian. "What do you know?"

Julian shook his head. "Nothing. Sorry. When my uncle isn't gardening or yelling at the neighborhood kids, he's sitting at the kitchen window, staring out while he listens to his police scanners. He knows everything going on in this little town." He looked down at his phone. "In fact, that's him right now asking if I think Teagan's guilty and telling me to be careful."

Teagan stared at her plate. "So, you heard, I'm a person of interest?"

He chuckled. "I don't believe it for a moment. You always seemed like such a sweet person. Why would the police question that?" Julian looked at her father. "Aren't you the police?"

"I am and because of that, I understand they have to follow every lead. Her name will be cleared in no time."

Julian twirled another long spaghetti noodle around his fork and then switched the fork to his other hand and ate the spaghetti.

How cool. Was he ambidextrous?

Julian twirled his spaghetti again with the same hand he'd eaten with, and then he switched hands again and ate a bite. He finished chewing and laid his fork down. "Do they have other suspects?"

"I'm not sure." Dad's mouth flattened. "For obvious reasons, I have to stay out of the investigation."

Julian looked at Teagan. "Can you think of anyone who might have hurt your friend?"

Teagan stared at the spaghetti on her plate. No one. Literally no one. Ty was the kindest person she knew. Sure, he aggravated her from time to time, but what best friends didn't disagree occasionally. "I wish I had seen the vehicle."

Dad tapped his fingers on the table. "Okay, so what do we do now? Let's think like the game of Clue. Who? Where? With What?"

"We know the Where: The parking lot." Teagan said.

Dad went to the game cabinet. He retrieved the game of Clue, laid the box in the middle of the table, and pulled out the board.

Aunt Connie scrunched her eyebrows. "Are we going to play right now?"

Teagan stood, understanding what Dad was doing. "No, we're going to use the board to piece all our clues together." She ran to the office, got scissors, sharpies, scotch tape, post-it notes, and cardstock, and then returned to the dining room. She tossed her armful on the table. "We know the crime happened in the parking lot with a vehicle, so now we need to find out who did it and with what vehicle."

She cut five pieces of cardstock into twenty squares. "As we come up with suspects and vehicles, we'll write them down."

Julian reached across the table for a marker and

wrote, *Ryan Dodger*.

Teagan raised an eyebrow at him. "How do you know Ryan?"

"Well, everyone in this area knows of the top point guard on FCs basketball team. Besides that, we know you didn't hit Ty, but according to my uncle the police think Ryan is a person of interest also, so—"

Teagan shook her head. "No. I can't imagine him having any part in this."

"How do you know?"

"Because I know him. He's one of my closest friends."

"Was he at the event when Ty got hit?"

He wasn't, but she didn't want to add fuel to Julian's fire. "He didn't do it."

"What kind of vehicle does he drive?"

She tilted her head and gave him a pointed look, pronouncing the sentence again slowly. "He didn't do it."

"What does he drive?" Julian didn't relent.

Who did this guy think he was, anyway? "Ryan drives a black truck, an F150, but I've seen his truck. No damage."

Julian wrote black F150 on a sticky note. "Those trucks bounce back. I have a buddy at school that hit a deer while he was driving fifty miles an hour. Not a dent."

Teagan put her hands on her hips. "Still, Ryan would never hurt Ty. Never. They are best friends."

"Teagan's right." Dad agreed. "Ryan could never do anything like that."

"Desperate times call for desperate measures. I've heard Ryan hasn't been hanging with the best of people lately."

"And how would you know that?" Teagan had had enough, and she was ready for Julian to leave.

"I'm not trying to upset you." He touched her hand, and she yanked it back.

He shrugged. "I promise, I'm trying to help. I told you my uncle hears a lot and watches a lot. He shares his theories with me night and day." Julian picked up another card. "And I think you ought to write down that missing girl's name."

"Lacey Brown? She's mean, but she's in love with Ty. I don't think she would hurt him." Teagan wrote Lacey's name on a card anyway.

"It is suspicious that's she's missing the day

after the hit and run though." Aunt Connie twirled spaghetti on her fork. "Could she be in hiding?"

"I guess that's better than the alternative. I don't like her, but I don't want anyone to have hurt her."

Dad cleared his throat. "Sounds like there are two crimes to solve."

"And the police think I'm involved in both."

"Ludicrous. Just ludicrous they could even think that." Dad shook his head.

"How about adding that baker with the childlike voice on your list of suspects," Julian chimed in. "Her bakery is just down the street, correct?"

"Betty? No way."

"Uncle Charles says she hides dead bodies in her basement. Maybe she took Lacey."

Teagan laughed. "Oh, my goodness. That's been the town joke for years. Your uncle can't possibly believe that's true. She's the sweetest woman around."

"Uncle Charles says she's crazy. He saw her going off on a teenage girl, maybe it was Lacey, the other day for—"

"He's one to talk. Just thirty minutes ago, he threatened the boy across the street and took the kid's kite because it landed in his yard. Maybe I should put your uncle's name on the list. He doesn't hide the fact that he doesn't like when Ty comes over." Teagan grabbed a card and wrote Mr. Lewis on it. "What kind of car does he drive?"

Julian stared at her.

"What. Kind. Of. Car. Does. He. Drive?"

"A gray Buick this week. Next week maybe his Tahoe or Corvette. He's a car connoisseur and has turned his old body shop at the Point into a garage where he stores them all. Look, he may be a mean, grumpy old man, but he's no murderer."

Dad leaned forward, his eyebrows pinched together. "No one said anything about murder."

Julian drew in a deep breath. "You're right of course, I guess I read too many detective novels. What we do know is that a girl is missing, and your best friend was hit by a car. Someone or maybe two someones are up to no good."

"That's obvious, Sherlock." Teagan scowled.

"All right, Teagan that's enough." Her father put his hands on the table. "We know this is hitting too close to home for you. Take a breath."

Aunt Connie stood, "Julian, thank you for

bringing the meal. It was very kind of you to join us." She moved to the front door and laid her hand on the knob.

Julian stood. "I'm sorry. I didn't mean to upset you. I really was trying to help and look at things from an outsider's opinion of the town and its people. You never really know anyone, you know."

Aunt Connie nodded. "That's true. I've been able to help on a case or two because I wasn't influenced by my relationship with the people of the town, but still, I think Teagan could use a break. It's been a long couple of days."

Julian patted Colonel Mustard on the way toward the door. He turned back for a second. "Forgive me."

Dad stood. "There are no hard feelings. It was nice meeting you and thank you for dinner."

"No problem."

Aunt Connie closed the door.

"You know he did make a few valid points." Dad suggested. "We are pretty close to the people in this town. But being a cop, I see people in a little bit more of a jaded light than you do. Think, Teagan. Sometimes, it's the most unlikely suspects who do the most unthinkable things. Who would have ever thought Lacey Brown would bully you like she did?"

"I wasn't surprised. But Betty and Ryan? Really? What motive would Ryan have? Ty beat him in a game of one on one? Those two would move mountains for each other. And Betty's got dead bodies buried in her basement? Ha. That's been hilarious since the rumor started."

"I know but sometimes the craziest of stories have some merit to them," Aunt Connie suggested. "The rumors about Bigfoot were laughable, too, until I was almost face to face with one."

Bigfoot? Had Teagan heard her right?

Dad jerked his head toward his sister, his eyebrows almost meeting his hairline. "Care to explain?"

She shook her head. "It's Polly's story to tell, but let's just say, I'm not too keen on camping anymore."

"When were you ever?" Dad laughed.

"Touché." Aunt Connie playfully smacked her brother's arm.

Teagan's stomach tightened. As interesting as a

Bigfoot story sounded, Teagan already felt too overwhelmed. "Betty's not some crazy psycho." Her mother's best friend had been her confidant and chief cheerleader in the time since Mom died.

"Maybe not, but maybe something unusual or illegal is going on in her bakery's basement." Aunt Connie suggested. "What do you think, Paul?" she asked, but then held up one hand and placed a finger to her lips with her other. Then she pointed. "I heard something," she whispered.

They remained quiet.

Even Colonel Mustard's ears twitched.

Something crashed from Teagan's room, and Colonel Mustard growled.

They all headed for the stairs at the same time, but Dad made them stay behind him.

"I left my window open," Teagan whispered. "Perhaps the wind blew something over."

"Perhaps." Dad cautiously made his way upstairs with them following. Only Colonel Mustard kept pace with him.

They rounded the corner and moved into the bedroom. "Hey, you!" Dad called.

Someone in dark clothes wearing a black face

mask crawled out Teagan's bedroom window onto the small roof.

Dad pushed past Teagan and into his room. In a second, he exited, gun in his hand. "Call 9-1-1!" He ran down the stairs and outside.

Teagan pulled out her phone as she watched from the window, but she felt like she was moving in slow motion. Colonel Mustard stood in the center of the room barking.

"Stop!" Dad's shout was followed by a crash.

A car engine revved and then a yellow Mustang raced down the street.

"Aunt Connie, I think the person just stole your rental."

Her aunt looked over Teagan's shoulder. "I don't have a rental. I took an Uber from the airport." She gasped. "Your dad's on the ground." She darted into the hall.

Teagan and Colonel Mustard followed, flung down the steps, and out the front door.

Dad moaned in pain.

Aunt Connie was already on the phone asking for an ambulance.

Dad raised himself up on his elbows. "I think I

broke my leg. Get Detective Evans. Ask for him specifically."

"Yes, Daddy." She pulled out her cell phone and dialed the police station. When she was directed to the detective, she held the phone to Dad's ear.

"Chase, someone just broke in my house. I sustained an injury while trying to pursue him. Yellow Mustang. Older model, 60s, maybe. Kentucky plates. I didn't get a number."

Teagan couldn't hear the reply, but from the sound of the other man's voice, he seemed to take the report seriously. Dad muttered some benign agreement and backed away from the phone.

Teagan ended the call. "Daddy, that car was at the YASO building about an hour before the fundraiser," Teagan advised. "I thought it was Aunt Connie's rental."

"Who was in the building at the time?"

"Me and Aunt Connie. Plus Mrs. Dodger, Betty, Marco, and maybe a few of their employees."

Dad lay slowly back toward the concrete. "I think we found the car that hit Ty. The front bumper was bent in."

Teagan helped Dad into bed and covered him with the blankets. "Are you going to be okay?"

"I'm fine, sweetie. A little broken leg isn't going to stop me. We're going to find out who did this and clear your name."

Aunt Connie placed a coffee on the nightstand next to the bed. "And I'm going to stay awhile to help around here if it's okay with you guys."

"Yes, please stay for as long as you like." Teagan hugged Aunt Connie.

"I do have another event coming up, but I'll stay as long as I'm able. Besides you know I can't pass up on the opportunity to solve a mystery."

"Mayhem does have a way of following you." He gave his sister a playful nudge with his elbow.

She elbowed him back. "That it does."

Teagan looked up at the ceiling. "So where do we start? We have no suspects except Julian's presumptions."

"Maybe we should look into them a little," Aunt Connie suggested. "It wouldn't hurt. Would it?"

"I guess not, and we could clear Ryan and Betty's name from any suspicions. And try to figure out what happened to Lacey."

Dad shifted in his bed. "Teagan, I don't like you being a part of this. It's dangerous."

"I'll be careful. I promise. I've watched the best my whole life." She squeezed his hand. "And I'll have Aunt Connie with me. The best amateur sleuth we know."

He leaned his head back against his pillow. "Okay. Start at the scene of the crime. Talk to everyone who was there when you remember seeing the Mustang. Take your pepper spray." He looked at Aunt Connie. "You, too. And promise me if anything starts to look hairy you two will get out of there."

Teagan waited for the detective and his crew to finish their sweep of her room, and then she went in, Colonel Mustard by her side. The police didn't find any evidence or clues to tell them why someone would be in her room. Everything looked perfectly normal. Not a thing out of place. Just the way she liked it.

She straightened her acceptance letter to UChicago hanging on her bulletin board as her stomach grumbled. The left-over garlic bread from dinner called to her. She turned to head out her door. "Come on, boy. Let's go get a snack."

Wait.

Her physics book was under her desk instead of on it. Maybe the police knocked it off when looking around for clues. Thank goodness, they hadn't torn her room apart. She picked up the book and a piece of paper fell out from it.

The words, *If you know what's good for you, you'll admit you did it,* were written in green and screamed at her from the note on the floor.

She snatched it, folded it, and slid it into her pants pocket.

Chapter Six

Backs Against the Wall

Teagan stood in the empty parking lot of the YASO building. She and Aunt Connie spread out a little on their hunt for evidence.

She crouched down and touched the spot where Ty's bloody body had lain. Now void of any evidence he'd been hit by a vehicle.

Aunt Connie stepped in behind her. "Do you remember seeing anything suspicious?"

Teagan shook her head. "No, not when I found Ty." Again, she looked at the place where he'd been lying. "I saw a few things a little earlier than that, though." She again went through the argument she'd seen between Ty and Lacey and how the girl had run off into the woods when Mrs. Dodger screamed inside the building.

"Mrs. Dodger was certainly easily alarmed." Aunt Connie scanned the woods on one side of the parking lot. "Where did you see that car you mentioned?"

Teagan pointed in the other direction. "The yellow Mustang was on the edge over there. I didn't recognize it, and it had Kentucky plates. That's why I assumed it was your rental from the airport. But with Louisville right across the river, I guess the car could have been one of the event workers who helped set up, but why would they hit Ty and drive off and why would someone with the same car break into my house?"

She touched her pocket where she'd put the letter she'd found in her room. *And why would they threaten me?* None of it made sense, but she couldn't tell Dad or Aunt Connie about it. Dad would certainly make her stop looking into it. And Aunt Connie would certainly tell Dad about the letter if she knew about it.

Aunt Connie motioned to the woods. "What I don't understand is why Lacey would run into the woods? Do you remember seeing her vehicle?"

"Now that you mention it. No. Her house is in that subdivision that backs up to the other side of these woods. Lots of people hike the trails to get from there to this part of town especially on nice weather days like yesterday. Lacey isn't the type to do that though, and she was dressed a little too nice for a hike. But who knows with her? I long stopped trying to figure out why Lacey does anything she does."

"Do you think she could have hidden in the woods and waited for Ty to return then hit him with the car?"

Teagan shrugged. "Like I've said before, she's a bully and vindictive, but I don't think she's capable of running over her boyfriend. And the Mustang doesn't add up either with the Kentucky plates."

"Maybe it wasn't the Mustang that hit Ty?" Aunt Connie walked toward the woods that marked the side and back of the property. "Come on. Let's take a look."

Teagan hopped up. "Should we wait until morning? It's getting dark."

"Just a quick look." Aunt Connie turned on the

flashlight on her phone. "Let's see if the police missed anything. I've got some bear spray too. Just in case." Aunt Connie held it up. "I'm always prepared."

Teagan held up her canister also. "Me too. You can never be too safe according to my dad."

Teagan followed her aunt into the woods as they shined their lights ahead of them. Everything was peaceful and calm. The night animals sang quietly. Something white, caught in a branch ahead of them, flapped back and forth in the gentle breeze.

Teagan removed the torn left corner of an envelope with the return address of Mrs. Dodger's friend's Travel Agency from the tree.

She held it up. "This is from part of the envelope that held the cruise voucher."

"Are you sure?" Aunt Connie took the paper from her and read it under the light.

Teagan pointed to a green scribble in the corner of it. "I wasn't thinking, and I accidentally marked the envelope when I was trying to get my favorite green glitter pen to work. I remember now. The voucher *was* on the auction table, inside the envelope. I didn't forget it at all."

"You were pretty busy getting things set up."

"Yeah, but if it was there, then when did it disappear and when was it returned? It wasn't there when Ty called me. I had just checked again."

"You think, maybe you overlooked it?" Aunt Connie was always one to be diplomatic in the way she said things.

Teagan looked at the pavement and thought it through. She could picture the empty spot on the table. "I don't think I did. I searched for it." She moved her gaze to meet her aunt's. "I think someone took it and then returned it."

"Why?"

She knew how ridiculous it sounded. It just didn't make sense. "I don't know."

Teagan's phone chimed with a text notification from Ryan.

> HEY. I HOPE YOU'RE OKAY. THIS IS ALL
> SUCH A MESS. I CAN'T BELIEVE THEY
> THINK WE'RE INVOLVED. INSANE.

"Is everything okay?" Aunt Connie directed her flashlight back toward the path.

"Yeah. It's from Ryan." She dialed his number, but it went to voicemail. "You know, he had been acting super weird the day before and the day of the fundraiser. He was almost angry about the cruise."

"About the cruise?"

"Yeah." Teagan veered around some undergrowth that her flashlight caught just before she walked into it. "Would he have removed the voucher and then felt guilty and returned it?" The second it was out of her mouth, she knew it didn't make sense.

"But why would he do that?" Aunt Connie asked.

Teagan shook her head. "I don't know."

Her phone vibrated. Another text from Ryan.

> *I can't talk now. Sorry. I can text though.*

Teagan texted him as she looked around while following Aunt Connie.

> Odd question. Did you pick up the cruise voucher and return it right before the fundraiser?

> *I wasn't there.*

He'd been there to talk with Ty. Didn't he remember that?

> You knocked me over when you came in.

YEAH, SORRY. I'D LEFT SOMETHING IN MOM'S OFFICE.

WHAT?

JUST A BOOK.

IN A HURRY?

Clearly, he was hiding something or was she just being too suspicious?

HAD TO GET IT TO THE LIBRARY BEFORE IT CLOSED.

His explanation would be reasonable if it weren't for the fact that Ryan hated to read. Plus, she remembered he'd told his mom he was late to the fundraiser because he'd been at Romeo Court. He wouldn't have had time to drop the book off at the library, drive by the park, let alone play a quick game of ball, and then get back to the gala at the time he'd arrived. He had to have lied to her or his mother. Her stomach knotted. Or maybe he had lied to both of them. Where had he been?

She paused beside a large live oak.

SO WHY DO THE POLICE THINK YOU'RE INVOLVED?

Sure, she believed Ryan was innocent, and clearly the police were wrong about her, but there was something else going on. She could tell.

   IDK. WHEREABOUTS AND SUCH. HOW ABOUT YOU?

  SAME.

  She wasn't sure why she didn't tell him more. The evidence they had on her was hearsay and involved the twisting of things she'd said. She had said it all though, whether she meant it or not. She understood the police had to investigate. But what did they have on him? Like he'd said, he was the class president, captain of the basketball team, and all-around great guy.

  She glanced up at the moon through the trees and switched off her flashlight. Aunt Connie had paused just ahead of her. *You know what's going on God. Can you help me figure it out?*

  The sound of sticks and leaves crunching further in the woods caught her attention. She pulled out her mace and looked around. Aunt Connie held her hands up in a gesture of *I don't know.*

  No sign of anything. It had most likely been an animal who'd already scurried away.

  Teagan's phone vibrated with another text notification. She read the message as she continued to walk.

*DO YOU THINK THEY REALLY BELIEVE
WE COULD BE INVOLVED?*

Teagan's foot bumped into something, tripping her and bringing her down on her knees hard. She dropped her phone and reached out to catch herself, falling onto something that wasn't wood, dirt, or leaves.

Something that felt very human.

She screamed and scooted backward and then in a frenzy felt around in the dark for her phone.

Aunt Connie turned and ran back to her. Her phone's light now illuminating the object Teagan had fallen on. Definitely human and not moving. A long-haired brunette lay face down. She wore the same outfit as Lacey the night of the fundraiser.

Teagan gasped. "Oh, Lacey!"

"You think that's the missing girl who bullied you?" Aunt Connie knelt beside her and touched Teagan's arm.

"Same." Teagan reached toward the figure on the narrow path.

"Don't . . . touch the body." Aunt Connie lifted both hands in her direction. "She's quite dead, and the police already think you're involved."

"I fell on her." Had she once again pointed blame to herself? Left fingerprints?

"It's okay. Just don't touch her again." Aunt Connie pushed buttons on her phone then put it to her ear. "We found a girl in the woods. I believe she's dead. We think it might be Lacey Brown."

Teagan sat on a nearby log, hugging her knees and rocking back and forth. What was going on in her small, little, safe town?

Red and blue lights swirled outside the woods. Two male paramedics, carrying a gurney, ran past Teagan and Aunt Connie to the female. One knelt beside her, pressed his fingers to her neck, and then checked her wrist. "No pulse."

The two paramedics looked her over further and then rolled her onto her back as her not-so favorite detective and three other police officers along with the town coroner approached Aunt Connie and Teagan.

"Evening ladies." Detective Evans tipped his head forward as he strode past them.

Teagan didn't know what to say so she remained silent. Aunt Connie did the same.

The final officer in the line was Gary Hensley, Dad's partner. "Hey, kiddo." He took one of the blankets tucked under his arm and wrapped Teagan in it. "You okay?"

She nodded.

Aunt Connie chimed. "I think she's in shock."

Gary held the other blanket out toward her, but Aunt Connie shook her head.

He knelt in front of Teagan and thumbed over his shoulder toward the opening to the woods "Your dad's waiting in my SUV in the parking lot. I didn't think he should be traipsing—

"I'm here, Teagan." Dad hobbled up the dark trail on his crutches.

"Paul, I told you to stay in the cruiser. What if you would have fallen?"

"There was no way I was going to stay and wait while my daughter and sister are out here."

"That's fine." Gary lowered his voice. "But I need you to stay out of the investigation. You are dad right now, not cop."

"I'll be on my best behavior." He held his fingers in the Star Trek Vulcan sign. "Scout's Honor."

Aunt Connie widened her eyes at Teagan and whispered, "See."

Teagan registered the motion but didn't respond. How could she? Her brain wasn't even functioning right now.

"Hey guys," Dad called to the paramedics. "Can one of you check my daughter?"

"Yes, sir." One of the men made his way toward her. He put on a fresh pair of gloves and looked her over.

Detective Evans moved back toward her, arms across his chest. "Is she good?"

"I'm . . . fine." Teagan shuddered and took a deep breath. "Besides falling on a corpse . . . I'm good."

The paramedic shined a light in her eyes. "Yes, no sign of injury or shock." He tucked the penlight into his shirt pocket and went back to the figure in the middle of the path.

The detective cleared his throat. "Good. I'm

going to need a DNA sample and fingerprints from Miss Wright."

Dad slipped one of his crutches between them. "Why?"

"Teagan fell on the body. I have to collect every ounce of possible evidence. Cory, Johnny, get on it."

"Yes, boss," Cory said first.

"Yes, boss," Johnny echoed.

Gary clenched his jaws and whispered to Dad. "I ain't calling him boss. Just cause he made detective he thinks he's a big shot."

"Excuse me, Detective Evans, is it? I was right here when it happened." Aunt Connie rose from the stump she'd rested on.

"You saw her fall?" He took out his phone and jotted a note with his thumbs flying over the keypad.

"Well, no. I was right over there." She pointed. "But I heard her cry out and turned around to find her on the ground."

"I see."

If Teagan was any judge of character, he didn't see what Aunt Connie had intended. And judging from her aunt's frustrated exhale, she knew it, too.

"This isn't Lacey Brown." The coroner hovered

over the girl's face. "Lacey's parents are friends of mine. This girl has a large birthmark across her left temple. Lacey doesn't. Though they do have a similar figure she doesn't really look like Lacey."

Teagan looked at Dad. "I never saw her face in the parking lot. I swore the girl arguing with Ty was Lacey. So, if that isn't Lacey then where is she? And who is that?"

Dad whispered. "I don't know, honey, but we will figure it out." He raised his voice to the coroner. "How long ago does it appear she died? Could her features—"

The detective whirled and glared at him.

"Fine. I won't ask questions."

"Good." The man turned away and kept his voice down. "This had to have happened recently unless someone dragged her body out here. My guys combed this area for hours after Ty's hit and run." His glance swung between Aunt Connie and Teagan. "What were you doing out here anyway?"

"Looking for clues to clear my niece's name. She's innocent." Aunt Connie answered a little too loudly.

The detective turned around to face them. "So,

you think you can do a better job than me and my guys." He directed his question toward Dad.

Aunt Connie stood and faced the man. "It doesn't hurt to take a look around. Clearly, you and your officers are on the wrong path, suspecting innocent kids."

"Innocent?" The detective scoffed. "Teagan has threatened a girl who's missing. And Ryan? Let's just say, he's not as perfect as everyone thinks."

What did he mean by that? "What do you have on him?"

The detective stared down at her. One of his officers called to him, and he turned away, but he wouldn't likely have told her anything anyway.

Dad's partner stood. "I can't share the details of an ongoing investigation. But if I were you, I'd keep my distance from Ryan." He punctuated the last part with a point in her direction.

"Officer Hensley," the detective called. Clearly, he didn't want anything to be shared. Not even kindness or comfort.

"There's something shoved in her mouth," the coroner said, probably louder than he'd intended. He used some long-handled tweezers to pull something white from her mouth.

Dad swung on his crutches toward the body. "What is that?"

"It's a piece of paper. Looks like . . ." The medical examiner uncrumpled it then showed it to the detective. The two men put their heads together.

Gary helped her dad back toward Teagan.

Detective Evans glanced at Teagan. "It's a certificate from the fundraiser to spend a day with Ty. The words *I told you to watch your back* are written in green glitter pen."

What? Teagan's heart hammered against her chest.

Aunt Connie looked at Teagan. "That's unusual. Not too many people can say they have a pen like that."

Teagan's stomach dropped. Did Aunt Connie suspect her now too?

"I'm going to have to tell the detective about your pen, Teagan." Gary's eyes were soft. "I can't ignore that I've seen you carrying it around all the time taking notes and such."

"Yes, but I didn't write that. In fact, now that I think about it, I haven't seen my pen since the fundraiser."

"Likely story." The detective moved into their group, coming between Dad and his partner. He exhaled and gritted his teeth. "And you just now noticed you haven't had your favorite pen. I mean how have you and Nancy Drew over here taken notes without it?"

"I guess I left it on the auction table with my clipboard. I've had other things on my mind the last couple of days."

The whole thing reminded her of the note she'd found. She touched her pocket to feel for the threatening letter. Maybe she should show them?

"Who purchased the day with Ty?" the detective asked.

"I don't know. I didn't stay. I went to the hospital."

Aunt Connie stepped forward and put her hands on Teagan's shoulders. "We didn't put it up for auction because we didn't feel it was appropriate. All things considered."

"What did you do with it then?" Gary asked.

"Mrs. Dodger took it. Put it in her office." She rubbed her hands up and down Teagan's arms.

"There's something else in the victim's mouth."
The coroner used his tweezers and pulled it out. "It's
a mutilated photo of Ty. His eyes have been poked
out and the words *die* are written in green across his
face."

Teagan's heart stopped. So, someone did want
Ty dead. She clutched her chest. *Why?*

The detective cleared his throat. "Who's the
girl, Teagan?"

Confused, she shook her head. "I don't know."

"Don't say another word, Teagan," Dad
warned.

She had a hard time catching her breath. "Why,
Daddy?"

"They think you did something to the girl."

Teagan pushed herself up to her feet, crossed
her arms over her chest, and glared at Detective
Evans. "I didn't do anything. Why don't you believe
me?"

He turned to Aunt Connie. "Why were you two
out here?"

"I told you. We were looking for clues."

He pointed his finger in Aunt Connie's face. "I
see you think you're quite the little sleuth. But

around these parts we don't need outsiders poking their nose in our investigations. We are top-notch."

Aunt Connie crossed her arms across her chest. "Not on this case obviously."

The detective grumbled under his breath and shouted toward Gary. "Get them out of here." He looked toward Dad. "And you, I mean it, you and your sister stay out of this." He pointed at Dad's chest. "You take your leave, heal that leg, and stay out of my investigation."

Dad straightened, lifting his weight off his crutches. "If you think for one minute that I'm going to let you railroad my daughter to try to put me in my place for questioning your competence as a detective, then you have another thing coming."

"You had no right to stick your nose into my promotion." The detective moved eye to eye with Dad.

"I can't trust a detective who will falsify documents. Even the minor ones." He leaned closer to the man and bobbed his head. "And I'm gonna find out who is doing all of this and framing my daughter for it."

Detective Evans sneered. "Good luck. It's

going to be impossible without the department backing you up."

Dad opened his mouth then shut it and motioned for Teagan and Aunt Connie to make their way out of the woods ahead of him.

"You sure you're okay?" Aunt Connie sat down next to Teagan on the porch swing, and Dad, leaning against his crutches, stood by the front door. Colonel Mustard barked inside.

"Hush," Dad called toward the door.

The dog stopped barking.

Okay? No, she definitely was not okay. She shook her head. "You know that I didn't write on that certificate or do that to Ty's pictures. Maybe someone took my pen or maybe it's a coincidence."

"Of course, we know that. It seems like someone is trying to frame you," Aunt Connie suggested.

"Why?"

"To throw suspicion off them." Dad looked

Teagan in her eyes. "I know you don't want to believe it, but Evans seems pretty sure Ryan is up to no good these days. He would know about your green pen, right?"

Teagan shook her head. "Yes, he knows about it, but I really don't believe he did any of this."

"Who else would know about your pen?" he asked.

"I don't know."

"Do you really carry it everywhere with you?" Aunt Connie questioned.

Teagan nodded.

Aunt Connie looked up at Dad. "Then anybody who knows her might have noticed she uses it."

"So, we're back to square one." Teagan ran her hand across the back of her head.

Dad swung his way toward her. "Don't you worry. We'll figure this out." He sounded more confident than she felt.

She slid her hand in her pocket and squeezed the note. She couldn't tell anyone about it now for sure. "But what if we can't figure it out."

"We will." He paused beside her swing.

"But what if—"

Dad laid his hand gently on her shoulder. "I won't rest until we clear your name, and you know Aunt Connie won't either."

Chapter Seven

Get Your Head in the Game

Yellow Mustang.

Teagan wrote the vehicle name on a card and laid it upon the Clue board alongside Betty's Van and Ryan's truck. She should toss those cards out. They weren't guilty, but she'd clear their names from any suspicion too.

The doorbell rang, and Teagan answered it. Julian held a plate of cookies toward her. "I come in peace. I'm sorry about yesterday. I'm hoping some Heavenly Bits O' Brickle cookies from Betty's bakery will help."

She couldn't resist his smile or Betty's cookies. "I guess I forgive you." She opened the door wider. "Come on in."

Colonel Mustard slid his head under Julian's hand, and he petted the dog. "At least someone's excited to see me." He looked around. "Where is everyone?"

"Aunt Connie ran to the store, and my dad's resting upstairs. Someone broke in last night and my dad—"

"Broke his leg, I heard."

Teagan raised her eyebrow.

"I told you my uncle hears everything. Right next door. Remember?" He pointed toward the house.

"I remember." She held out her hands for the plate of cookies.

His hand grazed hers as he gave it to her. He paused, allowing his hand to linger for a moment.

Colonel Mustard darted toward them, jumping up and knocking the cookies between them onto the floor. The furball then helped himself to them.

"Well, that's that." Julian laughed.

Teagan stuck out her lip. "Yeah, but I didn't even get one. They're my favorite."

"I know. Betty told me. She's as nice as you say she is."

"So, you don't think she's got dead bodies stored in her basement anymore?"

He grinned. "I'm not saying that. I just said she's nice." He put his hand on her arm. "You want to walk down to her bakery with me and get some more cookies?"

She could use some normalcy. "I'd like that."

She grabbed her cell phone from the coffee table, hollered up to Dad to tell him what she was doing, and then she followed Julian out the door and down the street toward the bakery.

"Uncle Charles said they found a dead female in the woods by YASO last night. Did you hear about it?"

"I'm actually the one who found her."

He halted and turned toward her. "You did?"

"We went to the YASO parking lot to try to piece together what happened. Then Aunt Connie wanted to look for clues in the woods. It was dark, and I was looking at my phone, I tripped over the body and landed on top of it."

"Did you freak out? I don't know if I could have held myself together if I fell on a dead corpse."

"I didn't sleep well, that's for sure."

"So, no idea who she is?"

"None."

"I'll let you know if Uncle Charles hears anything."

"Thank you."

Should she tell him the rest about the certificate and the photo of Ty? Probably not. That was all police stuff anyway.

"Have you heard anything about how your friend is doing? Is he still unconscious?"

Teagan shrugged. "His mom found a note that she thought was from me where I supposedly threatened him, so now she won't talk to me or let me see him. I have no idea how he's doing. It's amazing how few people are actually on my side in this."

"I believe you." He slid his hand into hers.

Was that okay? She barely knew him. She slid her hand away. "Thank you. I think you might be the only one besides my dad and aunt. Why do you believe me? You don't even know me."

"I just have a sense about people. It's a gift or sometimes a burden." He halted in front of the bakery door and looked in her eyes. "You're a good person, Teagan. You don't deserve what's happening to you."

"Thank you."

He opened the door, and they stepped inside. Betty greeted them with a wave. "Hello, guys. Julian, you back so soon?"

Teagan laughed. "It's Colonel's fault. He got a little excited when he smelled your Heavenly Bits O' Brickle cookies and knocked them all over the floor."

Julian chimed in. "And I wasn't about to let Teagan go without her favorite cookies."

"I see, but I hate to disappoint you. I sold you my last batch of the day."

Teagan looked down into the display case. "That's okay. Everything you have is delicious. How about an oatmeal raisin?"

"Will you have more tomorrow?" Julian asked. "She had her heart set on them."

Betty pulled the oatmeal raisin out of the display case and handed it to her. "I tell you what, today has been kind of slow. What if I teach you how to make them?"

Teagan smiled. "Yes, please."

"You promise not to share my recipe with anyone."

She held up her fingers in the Boy Scout symbol. She giggled to herself remembering how her dad and aunt always got it wrong. "Scout's Honor."

"Wonderful." Betty motioned for them to follow her behind the double swinging doors into her kitchen.

"Like I said sweetest person I know," Teagan whispered in Julian's ear.

He shrugged as if he wasn't sure he fully believed her.

Betty reached for a recipe box from a shelf with containers of flour, sugar, salt, sprinkles, and more. She flipped the box and pulled out a little yellow notecard. "This is my grandma's recipe."

"Thank you for sharing it with us."

Betty handed Teagan the card. "My grandma would make the Heavenly Bits O' Brickle every Christmas. She taught me everything I know. I miss her so much. You read off the ingredients, and I'll collect them."

Teagan did as she asked, pausing between each

ingredient while Betty ran around the kitchen grabbing the items.

When she had collected the last item, Betty stood by the oven. "Thank you, dear." She called Teagan and Julian to her side and gave them step-by-step directions until the batter was made and dropped onto the cookie sheets.

Betty placed them into two separate ovens and looked at Teagan and Julian. "Now we wait for them to bake."

Julian's phone rang. He stared at the caller ID. "Excuse me. I'm going to take this outside." He made his way out of the double doors.

Betty raised her eyes up and down in a playful manner. "You and Mr. Lewis's nephew, huh?"

"No, it's nothing like that. We're just getting to know each other."

"He seems pretty sweet on you."

"I guess. He's being really supportive through everything."

"The rumor on the street is that you're the one who hit Ty. Totally crazy, by the way."

"Yeah." She shook her head. "It wasn't me. I'm pretty sure it was someone with a yellow Mustang."

"Why do you think that?" Betty looked down at her phone and typed on it while she listened.

"It was parked outside at the fundraiser, and then someone sped off in one just like it last night after they broke into my house, and my dad chased them off. My dad said the fender was bent in."

"Oh, wow. Do the police have any idea whose car it is?"

"I don't think so. And did you hear about the dead girl in the woods?"

Betty raised her eyes and placed her hand on her heart. "Oh, my heavens. No. Who would have ever thought things like this would happen here."

"I'm sure you see lots of people drive by your bakery. I really think if we find the Mustang, we'll find who's behind all of this. Have you noticed anyone driving one? Especially, maybe yesterday when they were fleeing my house around five."

Betty shook her head. "No, I'm sorry I didn't. I haven't."

"That's okay."

Julian walked back inside.

"Everything all right?" Teagan asked.

"Yep, just my academic advisor. She was

asking when I plan to return. I don't know when that will be." He glanced down at the floor.

It had to be hard putting his life on hold, but to watch his uncle fading away had to be worse.

"It's good of you to be here for your uncle." Betty touched his shoulder.

He continued to stare at the floor, sadness in his eyes. He blew out a breath and then looked up. "When are these cookies going to be done?"

Betty glanced at the timer. "Eight minutes." Her phone dinged, and she looked down. "Oh, I need to take care of something in my apartment upstairs. I'll be right back." She ran through the double doors and then rushed back in. "I locked the front door and posted the I'll-be-right-back sign. Are you guys good to take the cookies out when they're done?"

"Yes, ma'am," Julian assured her.

"Let them sit a minute or two and then put them on the cooling racks. The racks are on the shelf over there by the basement door." Betty pointed. "It shouldn't take too long. My boyfriend just stopped by and needs to talk to me about something."

"Boyfriend?" Teagan raised her eyebrows up and down like Betty had done to her earlier. "Do tell."

"It's a new development. I'll fill you in later on all the details." Betty turned and went up a set of spiral stairs in the back of the room.

"That's exciting for her. She deserves happiness."

Julian made his way toward the shelves and reached for the cooling racks. "Hey, let's go check out her basement."

"No, let's not."

"Just a quick peek to be sure there aren't any bodies down there." He was being ridiculous.

"Ha. Ha. No."

Julian put the cooling racks back on the shelf, opened the door, and ran down the steps.

"Julian! No. Come back." She kept her voice as low as she could. "Shoot."

She went down after him. "Julian. Get back up here." She couldn't see anything. Total pitch black. "Julian come on. This isn't funny. Come upstairs."

She reached the floor, and someone grabbed her arm. She opened her mouth to scream but nothing came out. Her mace was hooked to her beltloop, but her limbs were heavy like cinder blocks from fear.

She froze *Come on, move. Move. Move. Move.*

The person pulled her further into the room and released her. Was it Julian? Did he think this was some kind of sick joke?

"Bwahaha." Julian held his flashlight from his phone under his chin, lighting only his face.

She yanked her arm away from him. "What was that for?"

Julian laughed. "You should have seen your face."

"It's not funny. Why would you do that?"

He touched her shoulder, but she flinched and backed away from him.

"Aw, I'm sorry. I was just trying to have a little fun. I mean the thought that dead bodies could be down here is kind of intriguing, don't you think."

"No. No. It's not. There are no dead bodies down here." She turned the flashlight on her phone and searched for a light switch. She found a light pull string hanging from the ceiling and yanked it. She pointed at the stone walls, dirt floor, and open ceiling. "See, an everyday old building basement. Kind of creepy but no dead bodies. Let's go back upstairs."

"It looks like this is her home office." He made his way to the desk against the wall and picked up a stack of papers then laid them down and proceeded to look at other items on her desk.

"Yep. Let's go upstairs." It wasn't right being down here. She turned to head up the steps.

"What a cool pen. I've never seen a green one before." He examined it in his hand.

She stepped closer to get a better look. It was exactly like hers. Gold on the top and bottom with the middle of the pen a sparkly green. It had to be a coincidence. Betty wouldn't steal her pen and set her up. Would she?

"Hey Teagan, look at this." He pointed to a shelf.

"What about it?"

"Look at the floor. See how the dirt is in a perfect line from the shelf being moved. It's got to be one of those hidden doors."

He slid the shelf along the line opening the wall to another room.

"What are you doing?" Betty shouted behind them.

Teagan's heart skipped a beat. "I'm sorry. We

shouldn't be down here."

"You're right. You shouldn't be." Betty put her hands on her hip.

"It's my fault. I've heard the rumors of dead bodies, and I—" Julian started.

Betty pointed her finger in his face. "I'm so sick of that. At least once a month some teenager tries to break into my basement to prove I'm crazy. The only thing I have stored down here is bulk baking supplies and other business odds and ends. You are just like the rest of them. Teagan, I'm shocked at you."

"It's not her fault. She tried to convince me to not come down here."

"But you came down here anyway." Betty raised her voice.

"Only to stop him."

"What's with the secret room? What do you keep in there?" he questioned.

"Julian, stop being nosy." Teagan could slap him upside the head.

"Nothing," Betty answered.

"The shelf appears to have been moved a lot. See how the floor is worn there."

"It's a safe room."

"You use it a lot?" he asked.

"Only for tornado warnings and such. I don't like going in there because I'm afraid of spiders. Look I don't have to answer to you. You're in my basement uninvited. I want you to leave now." The faint sound of the cookie timer beeped. Betty pointed up the stairs. "Leave or I'm calling the cops."

"I'm so sorry." Teagan pleaded as she followed Julian up the stairs.

Betty pressed her lips together and stomped up the steps.

"Betty, really. Please forgive me."

Betty wouldn't look at her and paused to turn off the timer. "Just go," she all but whispered.

Teagan slumped her shoulders and exited the building.

Julian jumped and clapped his hands. "That was awesome!"

"No, it wasn't. What is wrong with you?"

"That really got the adrenaline going."

"You got one of my favorite people mad at me. I told you not to go down there." What had he been thinking?

"I think she's lying. We should totally sneak back in there and see what's in her safe room. She was awful angry and defensive."

Was he crazy? "Maybe because it's like she said. She's tired of people breaking into her basement." She turned on him and planted her hands on her hips. "Would you want random people breaking into your house and invading your privacy. I can tell you it's no fun. It's scary and you can't sleep, terrified they are going to come back and what they might do the next time. Ugh, I can't believe you did that. What's wrong with you?"

He shrugged and held up his hands. "Okay, you're right. I'm sorry."

"I'm going home, and I don't want you walking with me." Teagan put her hands across her chest. "And don't show up on my doorstep tomorrow with dinner or cookies to try to smooth things over." She turned and walked across the street.

"Hey, Teagan. Look." His call was full of surprise.

Teagan hesitated. Nothing would give her more pleasure than to keep walking, but Julian sounded different. She turned back toward him. "What?"

He pointed at a car squeezed into the parking spot between the wall of the bakery and Mrs. Dodger's blue van. A yellow Mustang.

Crouched behind a half wall across the street from the bakery, Teagan and Julian spied over the top waiting for the driver of the Mustang to return. Teagan looked down at the time on her cell phone: 8:43 p.m.

"Do you think it's Betty's car?" Julian asked.

"No, she didn't seem fazed when I mentioned the car. Besides, the person who broke in my house had to be fairly fit to get away from my dad and down the side of the house and to their car that quick. No offense, but Betty isn't exactly light on her feet."

"What about her boyfriend?"

Maybe. That could explain the green pen in Betty's basement. That seemed more plausible than sweet Betty. Maybe her boyfriend did own the

Mustang, took the pen, and was framing Teagan, but who was he?

She stretched her neck to the left and then the right and groaned. Crouching for so long was taking a toll on her body.

"If you want to go on home. I don't mind staying." Julian put his hand on her back.

She flinched. "That's okay."

"I am sorry, you know, for making Betty mad at you. Like I told you I just have a sense about people, and something's off about her."

Teagan had heard enough of his theories.

The door to the bakery opened. Betty and a tall, thin, black-haired man exited.

"That's Marco from the Italian Bistro." He was the new boyfriend? He certainly seemed attentive.

And he was the perfect build for the intruder. Teagan didn't know him well, though. Only through his catering at YASO events and her eating a few times at his restaurant. Could he be hard-hearted enough to kill someone and frame her? Surely not.

Betty giggled at something as he bent down to kiss her.

"I'm sure their dinners together are amazing."

Julian exclaimed.

"Shh." Did he want her to get caught again?

Oh sorry, he mouthed.

The couple rounded the corner into the parking lot. Betty looked around. Teagan ducked down lower.

"You like it." Marco pointed to the Mustang.

"Where did it come from?"

"From one of the guys at my restaurant. He told me I could take it for a spin for a few days."

Betty looked around. "Who?"

"You don't know him. He's new."

"Who let you borrow it, Marco?" she demanded.

"Pedro. Okay. His name is Pedro. He just moved here from Louisville. He used to be a chef at Churchill Downs."

Betty looked around again.

"When did he give it to you?"

"This morning. He got it all cleaned up and detailed real nice so I could take my lady out on the town for a nice evening."

"Give it back. Now. Call him and tell him to come get it now."

Marco shook his head. "Why are you freaking out?"

She lowered her voice to a volume Teagan couldn't hear.

"Your friend, Teagan, must have seen one like it." Marco walked to the front of Mrs. Barker's van and looked at the sports car. "Look no dents in the bumper. It must be another Mustang."

"It's more likely he got it fixed and is having you drive it around to deflect attention off himself."

"You really think Pedro had time to replace a bumper that quickly."

"I don't know. In this day and time with same day and next day delivery, maybe he had time to fix it. Either way, I don't want you driving it around. The police are looking for a yellow vintage Mustang. How many do you think are in Floyds Knobs? Probably, just this one."

"So, because Teagan, the number one suspect in all of this, told you she saw a car similar to this one racing away from her house, you believe Pedro broke into Officer Wright's home?"

"She said a yellow Mustang was at the fundraiser that night too." Betty clasped and unclasped her hands.

He stared at her. "So now, it was the one that hit Ty as well?"

"Wasn't Pedro helping you at the fundraiser?"

"Yeah, but why would some fresh-out-of-culinary-school kid who just moved here from across the river want to hurt Ty?"

Betty shrugged. "Maybe it was an accident and he freaked out. I don't know. You need to talk to him."

He touched her elbow. "Okay. I will."

Betty sighed. "Also, a girl's been found dead in the woods." Her voice had a shaky sound to it.

"What?" The man spun and faced her. His reaction sure seemed sincere, but Teagan had been fooled before.

"Yeah, found her last night. And Lacey Brown's still missing. Don't you see, you can't be found driving that car. This is all so crazy." She turned toward the bakery door.

"Where are you going?"

She whispered to him, and they went inside.

Teagan looked at Julian. "Let's go. I'm done spying on her. We've invaded her privacy enough today. Your Spidey-tingle is obviously off. Betty and Marco didn't have a clue about the car."

Julian shrugged. "I guess, but something still doesn't feel right."

Betty and Marco exited the bakery. Betty held something under her arm. The two rushed to the Mustang, and Betty fanned out an off-white sheet. They hurried to cover the car and then got in her van and drove off.

Teagan ducked down as Betty passed, but Teagan was able to see that the back bumper was dented in. The van turned the corner out of sight.

The Visitor Plays a Game

Chapter Eight

In Her Corner

"Lay down, boy." Teagan told Colonel Mustard who had paced back and forth across the living room floor for the past fifteen minutes.

Aunt Connie, wearing a robe and holding a mug of coffee, came out from the kitchen and stopped at the dining room table. She looked over the clue cards and then made her way to the couch and plopped onto it next to Teagan. "Morning. You're up early."

"Morning. Yeah, crazy Colonel woke me up with his insistent bark at my closet. Ended up it was a ladybug." Teagan laughed. "He's a great watch dog, but does it have to be at seven thirty on a Saturday morning?"

"A ladybug?" Aunt Connie took a sip from her mug. "In your spotless closet?"

"It was on the door. But after this weekend, there could be a huge tarantula in there and I wouldn't know. I haven't opened my closet since the night of the gala." She looked down at her yoga pants and t shirt—the same outfit choice from her chest of drawers she'd made the last few days since coming home from the police station.

"I see you added a new name. Pedro? And you have the Yellow Mustang sitting with it. Did you find some more clues?"

Teagan nodded. "I believe so."

"Who's Pedro?"

"Remember the caterer from the fundraiser?"

"His name was Pedro? I thought it was Marco."

"It is. Pedro works for Marco. Apparently, the yellow Mustang belongs to Pedro, and he let Marco borrow it. Get this, though, no dent in the Mustang. But guess whose vehicle does have damage?" Teagan took a breath and tapped Betty's card. "Her van's back fender has a fresh dent."

"Do you think she hit Ty?"

"I can't imagine her doing anything like that."

Teagan sighed, but there was still a question without an answer. "She has a green glitter pen, though. It's exactly like mine. I mean exactly."

"You sure?"

"Positive. My mom gave me a set of fifteen glitter gel pens a few months before she died. Remember she was such a wonderful artist. We loved to draw together. Anyway, I choose one pen a year to use. This is the year of green. These pens are fancy with gold at the top and at the bottom and so was the one on Betty's desk. I mean, seeing a green pen isn't necessarily alarming. But the same kind is, especially, when her van is dented in, and someone is leaving notes in a dead girl's mouth using a green pen."

"That does seem suspect." Aunt Connie's eyebrows ruffled together.

"But I know Betty. She was my mom's best friend, and she's been like a mom to me since I lost mine. I don't know how to explain the pen or damage to the back of her vehicle, but there must be an explanation. She would never hurt anyone or frame me."

Aunt Connie took a sip of her coffee. "I hope

so. Maybe you can talk to her, ask her about the pen and what happened to her van."

That would be tough. "I can't. She's pretty upset with me because Julian is stupid." She explained to her aunt Julian's idiocy and how angry Betty was.

"Betty will forgive you. I'm sure."

Teagan shrugged. "I hope so."

Colonel Mustard got up from his bed and went to the front window. He whined and then paced in the living room again. Teagan looked out the window but didn't see anything.

"You gotta go out, Colonel?" Teagan asked.

He barked. She followed him to the back door and opened it. Barking, he darted into the yard chasing a squirrel up a tree.

"Leave that innocent squirrel alone."

Footsteps hit the pavement on the driveway that ran next to the yard. Colonel Mustard dropped his front paws to the ground and ran to the fence, whining. Julian passed the house and stopped at the fence.

He leaned over and petted Colonel Mustard. "Hey, boy." In his opposite hand he held a rose. "I know you told me not to come knocking on your door with dinner or cookies, but you didn't say anything about your backyard or flowers."

She gritted her teeth together. The giddy first impressions she'd had two days ago had quickly faded, and she truly wanted nothing to do with him anymore. "Your charming ways don't work here."

He pouted. "Ah, come on. I'm not trying to be charming. I'm just asking for a little forgiveness. You know the Bible says you're supposed to forgive."

She didn't answer. How could she? He was right. She lifted her gaze to his.

His smile spread from ear to ear. He held the rose out to her. "What do you say? Forgive me?"

She shook her head. *No way.*

"Really. Come on. Forgive me. Say you'll go with me to Marco's tonight. We can do more detective work and look into this Pedro."

"No." She crossed her arms across her chest. She didn't need him. "Come on, Colonel. Let's go in." She made her way toward the door.

"I walked by the bakery this morning. The Mustang is gone."

She halted before she reached the steps and slowly turned back to him. "It's gone?"

"Yep. And it might just be because I made an anonymous tip to the police."

"You called the police?" He seemed determined to make trouble for Betty.

He gave her an innocent look. "You wouldn't want a criminal to get away, would you?"

She stormed into the house with Colonel Mustard and slammed the door. "Oh, that guy infuriates me."

Aunt Connie set her coffee on the end table and stood. "Who."

"Julian. He thinks he's so smooth."

"What did he do?"

"Brought me a flower."

Aunt Connie covered her mouth and widened her eyes. "Oh, how awful."

"I don't have time for his nonsense."

"You know he was only trying to help you find answers. I've also found myself in an uninvited location a time or two looking for clues."

"Well, I don't need Julian or his Spidey-tingles."

Aunt Connie furrowed her brows. "His what?"

"He says he's good at reading people. That's how he knows I'm not guilty."

"He's not wrong there."

Teagan couldn't argue with that. "But he's convinced that Betty is. I'm tired of his assumptions about my friends." She went to the table and picked up the cards with Ryan's and Betty's names. "We're going to figure this out." She pointed back and forth between Aunt Connie and herself. "Thank you for being here. I'm glad I've got you."

Aunt Connie side hugged Teagan. "That you do. And don't be so hard on Julian. He's only trying to help."

"I know, but he just makes me so mad." She glanced down at the cards she held.

"Boys can have a way of doing that to us."

Teagan tilted her head backward and let out a small laugh. "Isn't that the truth." She tossed the cards into the can beside the table. She shouldn't have added them in the first place. The tension and frustration eased a bit. "Will you go to lunch with me at Marco's Italian Bistro? I need to see what we can find out about Pedro."

"Sure. I'll go get ready." Aunt Connie carried her coffee mug to the kitchen.

Colonel Mustard sat at the front window. He propped his head against the sill and wagged his tail.

"What are you looking at, Colonel?"

Julian stood in front of his uncle's house, talking to Detective Evans. It looked friendly enough and the conversation ended with a handshake and a wave. What could the detective have wanted from Julian? Possibly more information about what he saw at Betty's? But didn't Julian say he'd called in an anonymous tip?

Detective Evans got in his car and drove away. Julian looked around, and Teagan took a step away from the window. Julian pulled out his phone and typed on it.

Colonel Mustard whined again. She ruffled her dog's ears. "You really like that guy?"

Colonel Mustard panted, wagging his tail and keeping watch of Julian. If her beloved dog adored the guy, could she have made a mistake about him?

Julian turned and caught her looking at him. He waved and walked toward her porch.

She bit her bottom lip. Now she'd have to talk

to him again. She opened the door and Colonel Mustard rushed out to him, greeting Julian at the bottom of the steps.

Julian crouched down and petted the animal, and it licked his face.

"You do have a way with dogs." Teagan closed the screen door.

"How about beautiful ladies, like yourself."

He definitely knew how to put on the charm.

"Forgive me. I promise I was only trying to help." He held his hands together in a plea.

He had only been kind to her. Sure, he'd done a few stupid things, but what guy hadn't been foolish on occasion? If Colonel Mustard had a good sense about him, he couldn't be all that bad, could he?

"I saw you talking with Detective Evans. Everything good?"

"Yes. Chase . . . I mean Detective Evans is one of the few friends my uncle has in this town. He was checking in on him."

"Oh, that's nice."

"Yeah. He's a good guy." Julian clicked his cheek.

For a person who claimed to have a sense about

people, Julian's Spidey-tingle seemed to be off. According to Dad, Detective Evans didn't play fair when it came to promotions or investigations, and the way he'd talked to her was anything less than kind. Maybe the detective was a better person off the field than on it.

"How is your uncle doing?" Teagan took a step forward.

"He's hanging in there. Each day is different. Today's been a hard one."

"I'm sorry."

"Thank you. He's resting now. Should sleep for several hours. I'm going to head back to my apartment after I catch a bite to eat."

Julian truly was a caring person. She should give him another chance. "My aunt and I are going to Marco's for lunch. You want to join us?"

"Yeah, I'll meet you there."

"See you in a bit, then."

He waved and then walked to his uncle's porch.

She went back inside and closed the door. Colonel Mustard nuzzled against her side. "I love you, buddy." She bent down on her knees. "You're a good boy."

"Hey, Teag," Aunt Connie called from upstairs.

Colonel Mustard barked.

"Shh. Yes, I'm downstairs."

Aunt Connie, wearing a red blouse, skinny jeans, and a pair of red heels, came to the top of the steps. "Do you have a pair of earrings I can borrow? I dropped one of mine down the drain." She turned her palms upward. "So frustrating when I do things like that. I knew I shouldn't have laid them on the counter."

So, her aunt did make mistakes every once in a while. "Sure, I have the perfect pair to match that outfit."

She made her way upstairs. Aunt Connie and Colonel Mustard followed her into the room. Her dog growled at the closet door. "Remember, we found the ladybug earlier. I tossed it out the window." She petted him. He stopped growling and sat, staring at the closet.

She went to her jewelry box, opened the top drawer, and pulled out a black velvet box. "These were my mom's. Beautiful square-cut diamonds. I only wear them occasionally."

"The ones you wore to the fundraiser?"

"Yes, those."

"Oh, I remember. They were beautiful."

Teagan opened the box and froze.

"Thank you for—" Aunt Connie started. "What's wrong?"

"My mom's earrings aren't here."

"Are you sure you returned them?"

"I'm positive. Right after I got home from the hospital."

"A lot has happened since then. Could you maybe have forgotten to put them away."

"I didn't. I'm like you. I don't like things out of place. I wouldn't have left them laying around. Besides, after the police did a sweep of my room, I checked everything too. The earrings were there."

"And you haven't worn them again?"

"No."

"I'm sorry we couldn't find the earrings." Aunt Connie slid into the booth across from Teagan at Marco's Italian Bistro.

Teagan frowned. "What upsets me the most is they belonged to my mom. How do they just go missing? I hate to think that someone was in my room again. And why would someone want my mom's earrings?"

"What about your mom's earring?" Julian asked as he slid into the booth next to her.

"I'm sure it's nothing. I probably misplaced them, but has your uncle noticed anything unusual in the neighborhood, particularly my house the last two days?"

"He hasn't mentioned it, but like I told you earlier he isn't feeling too well. He's been in bed or on the couch mostly."

Aunt Connie frowned. "I'm sorry to hear that."

"Thank you. He's got a rough road ahead of him."

Teagan patted his hand. "He's lucky to have you."

Claire Stein, wearing a black apron, stepped up to the table. She glared at Teagan as she handed them menus. "Afternoon. I'll be your waitress. Can I get you something to drink?"

"A cola," Julian answered.

Aunt Connie tapped the table. "Water would be perfect."

"Water." Teagan placed her menu on the table. "How are you doing, Claire? Is there any news about Lacey?"

Claire, clearly frustrated, shook her head and blew out a long exhale. "I will give you guys a few minutes to look over the menu. I'll be back soon."

She headed toward the kitchen.

"That was Lacey's best friend."

Julian squinted. "Lacey is the missing girl, correct?"

Teagan nodded.

Aunt Connie smirked. "She was giving you the evil eye, that's for sure."

"She probably thinks I have something to do with Lacey's disappearance and that I hit Ty." Teagan surveyed the room. "The majority of people most likely assume the same."

Julian shook his head. "No way. If they know you even a little, they could never believe that."

A Hispanic young man wearing a chef jacket, pants, and apron came to the table with a tray of glasses. He handed their drinks to them. Aunt

Connie put her hand on her glass. "Thank you, Pedro."

He furrowed his brows as he looked at Julian. "You're welcome."

Aunt Connie pointed to his apron. "Your nametag."

He looked away from Julian and touched his nametag. "Oh, yes. I forget that. I'm normally back in the kitchen, but today I'm visiting each table to meet our guests. Can I get you guys anything else?"

Aunt Connie looked down at the menu. "I'm visiting from out of town. What's good here?"

"The shrimp fettuccine is amazing. Chef Marco's special sauce is to die for."

Aunt Connie let out a small laugh. "That does sound lovely. Thank you."

"You're welcome."

"How long have you worked here?" Aunt Connie gave her award-winning smile. She had a way about her that could make anyone feel comfortable and tell their life story.

"About a month ago. I was a line chef at Churchill Downs for years, but Chef Marco has brought me in to train as a sous chef."

"That's wonderful." Aunt Connie's expression glowed with enthusiasm. "The owner's a pretty good guy, huh."

"Seems to be." Pedro looked toward the kitchen while fidgeting with the string of his apron.

"Marco donated the meal for the fundraiser we . . ." Aunt Connie pointed to herself and Teagan. ". . . organized for Young Athletes Scholar Organization. Now that I think of it, you look super familiar. Did you help that night? You have a yellow Mustang, right?"

His eyes darted toward the kitchen again. "No. What? I'm sorry. What did you say?"

"Did you help at the fundraiser the other night?" Julian repeated Aunt Connie's question.

Pedro glanced at Julian and then back to Aunt Connie. "Yes, ma'am. It was a nice event . . ." He looked at Teagan and then at the floor. "Er . . . Well, I mean that boy getting hit was awful, but the actual event was nice. I got several autographs."

"That's cool. Whose autographs?" Julian asked.

"Roland Langley from the Brooklyn Bouncers was my favorite."

Julian eyes widened. "No way. That's

awesome." He spoke to Teagan. "I didn't know you had connections like that?"

"Actually, Mrs. Dodger does. Her brother, before he passed, connected with tons of athletes over the years and had an unbelievable amount of support from people like Roland Langley. The gala brings in people from all over the country who attend every year to give to YASO and mingle with celebrities and athletes."

"And this year's fundraiser did very well," Aunt Connie chimed in. "Even with the circumstances."

Chef Marco stepped in next to Pedro. "Afternoon, Teagan, Connie, sir. Everything okay?"

Aunt Connie placed her hands on top of her menu. "Fantastic. We were asking Chef Pedro what's good, and then we started chatting with him about the fundraiser the other night."

"All things considered it was a wonderful evening." Marco looked at Teagan. "I'm sorry to hear about what happened to Ty. Just awful. I hear the doctors think he might pull through though."

Teagan's heart soared. Oh, thank goodness. It was awful not knowing anything. Ty had to wake up. He had to be okay. "Thank you. I hope so."

"I enjoyed the chicken marsala you served at the gala, and Julian brought us some yeti spaghetti the other night. Fantastic." Aunt Connie motioned to Teagan and Julian. "I'm looking forward to trying something else. Oh, do you know Julian?"

Marco held out his hand to Julian. "I don't believe we've met. Nice to meet you."

"Likewise." Julian returned the handshake.

Marco spoke to Pedro. "I need you in the kitchen."

Pedro turned to them once again and gave a sharp nod. "It was nice to meet you all." He turned and moved toward the back of the restaurant.

"Your waitress should be right with you to get your order." Marco pointed toward them. "Can I get anything else for you guys while you wait?"

"Actually," Aunt Connie spoke up, "Can you bring us a couple-two-three garlic breadsticks?"

"Yes, ma'am. I'll have your waitress bring it right out. Enjoy your meal." Marco left the table.

"Shoot. We didn't get a chance to ask Pedro about the Mustang again." Teagan lowered her voice.

"We'll find a way to talk to him again, but I

don't get a burglar or murderer vibe from him, but Marco on the other hand . . ." Julian whispered.

Teagan shook her head. "Julian thinks he has a sixth sense about people."

"It's my superpower."

"I see. That is a good asset to have." Aunt Connie took a sip of her water. "I have a bit of that myself. It's come in handy over the years. Teagan's pretty good at reading people too." She looked at her. "What feelings did you get."

Teagan tapped her glass with her fingernails. "Pedro seemed nice enough, but he was nervous."

Aunt Connie snapped her finger and pointed at Teagan as if she was on to something. "I noticed that."

"Yeah, but maybe he's just an anxious person." Julian shrugged, keeping his voice low. "Like a dog who always has his tail between his legs for no reason. Unlike Marco who thinks he's an alpha. I don't trust the guy."

"Really? I don't get a bad sense about Marco," Aunt Connie whispered.

Julian winked. "That's because you're being influenced by his chicken marsala."

"Ha. Ha." Aunt Connie smirked. "Maybe, but have you had it? It's fabulous."

Claire returned to the table with a scowl on her face. "Are you guys ready to order?"

"It can't be that bad, can it?" Julian grinned, putting on the charm.

Claire glared at Teagan. "What's that mean?"

"You look so angry. Why?" Julian asked.

Claire pointed at Teagan. "Ask her."

"What did I do?" Teagan shrugged.

Claire put her hands on her hips. "Don't play dumb. You hit Ty, and then you did something to Lacey." She raised her voice. If anyone didn't already know about the speculation that Teagan was involved, they most certainly did now.

"I didn't, Claire. I swear."

"Everyone thinks you're so sweet, but I know you aren't. Lacey told me all the awful things you've said to her."

"That was after she bullied me and spread lies all over social media about me. I was hurt and mad and embarrassed. I'm ashamed of myself for threatening her. That's not me. I'm sorry I said those things. I didn't mean them."

"I heard you threaten her the other night too. Right before you hit Ty with your car. You were so jealous of them. You wanted Ty all for yourself."

"Not true, Claire. But I do believe he deserves someone who will love and treat him with kindness. Lacey was always bossing him around."

"So, he should be with someone like you, right?" Claire smirked.

"No, it's not like that. He's like my brother."

"Yeah right. You're lying. Just like you were lying about hitting Ty and doing something to Lacey."

"I'm not lying. I want to help find her. Do you know anything that might help?"

"You don't want to help." Claire put her order pad in her apron's pocket.

Aunt Connie slid to the edge of the booth and put her hand on Claire's arm. "I know you're worried about your friend. I'm telling you my niece had nothing to do with Lacey's disappearance or Ty's hit and run. We really do want to help. Let bygones be bygones."

"What?" Claire snarled and took a step back.

"Let what happened in the past stay in the past."

Aunt Connie's voice remained calm. "We want to help. I'm pretty good at solving mysteries. This isn't my first rodeo. Help us find her? What do you know?"

Teagan spoke softly. "I'm really sorry for everything I ever said about Lacey. It's no secret that I don't like her, but I don't want anything bad to happen to her. We used to be really close a long time ago. And Ty is my best friend. I promise you there is nothing romantic there at all. Just like you love Lacey, I love Ty. I couldn't hurt him. Ever. No matter what dumb stupid things I've said in the past."

"You promise me? You had nothing to do with any of it?"

Teagan shook her head. "I swear."

"I'm just so worried. First Ty. Then that girl in the woods. And Lacey's still missing. This is something you might expect down the hill, but not up here in the Knobs."

Aunt Connie touched Claire's hand. "We are going to do our best to find her."

"Okay. It's against my better judgment, but I'm going to trust you all." Claire whispered as she looked around, "We can't talk here. Meet me at the library at five."

A police cruiser sat outside Mr. Lewis's house as Teagan, Aunt Connie, and Julian made their way up the street from their lunch at Marco's. Julian froze. Teagan joined him. Aunt Connie continued moving down the street.

"I can't go up there." Julian stared at his uncle's house.

"Why?" Teagan touched the side of his arm.

"What if he's dead? I left him alone. I wouldn't be able to live with myself." He dipped his chin into his chest.

"If it was a problem with your uncle, it would be an ambulance, not a cruiser. Let's see what's going on."

He sighed. "Okay."

As Teagan reached her own house, she spotted Mr. Lewis on his porch swing. His dog, a Pitbull, lay at his feet, and Officer Gary stood on the second step with his arms across his chest talking up to Mr. Lewis.

"Looks like your uncle's fine." Teagan motioned toward the porch.

"Yeah, but why are the police talking to him?" His face turned pale, and he bit at his bottom lip.

"Let's find out."

"I'll go get your dad." Aunt Connie peeled off as Dad, on his crutches, came out Teagan's front door. They joined Teagan and Julian on the sidewalk in front of his house.

The dog raised his head, yawned, and laid his head back down. Gary turned and glanced at Teagan and Julian's hands. He shook his head, and then gave a nod to Dad. "Paul."

"Hey, partner. Everything okay?"

Gary raised his brows and turned toward Mr. Lewis. "Thank you for your help. We'll stay in touch if we have any further questions."

Mr. Lewis stood. "Sure thing. Come on, Killer. Let's go in." He opened his screen door and the dog followed. Then he shut the door.

Gary walked through the yard to Dad. "Paul, can we talk at your house?"

"Yeah, sure. Come on in." Dad motioned for him to follow him to the front door.

Teagan gave Julian a smile. "See your uncle is fine. Are you okay?"

"Yeah, but what was that all about?"

"I don't know. Why don't you go ask your uncle and I'll head on into my house and see what I can find out too. Then we can meet up later at the library."

"Sounds good." He turned to go inside.

"Hey, since when did your uncle have a Pitbull named, Killer."

"He's mine. I can't have him at the apartment."

"But you could have him in the dorms at school?"

Julian shook his head. "No, I lived in a house in Louisville."

"Louisville? I thought you went to school at UChicago?"

"What? Did I say Louisville? That's weird. I meant Chicago. I've been considering transferring to UofL so I can stay close to Uncle Charles and finish school. Louisville must be on my brain."

"Must be. It would be nice if you could finish

up school here."

"Yeah, but it would be nice if we could go to school together in Chicago, too." He reached for her hand.

She squeezed his hand. He was growing on her. "I think I would like that." She glanced at her door. "I better go on in."

"Yes, we'll meet up later."

He let go of her hand and went inside his house as Teagan made her way through her yard. Colonel Mustard greeted her right inside the door.

"Hey, Colonel." She patted his head.

Satisfied with the attention, Colonel Mustard went to his bed, spun a circle, then lay down. Teagan took a spot between Dad and Aunt Connie on the couch.

"So, you and the Lewis boy are a thing?" Gary asked from the recliner—his usual spot when he visited.

"No. Just friends."

"That's not what it looked like." He glanced toward the dining room table, then stood and went over to it. "What do you have here?" He picked up a card. "Lacey?" Then he read the rest. "Pedro?

Yellow Mustang? Mr. Lewis? Garage of cars at the Point? Is this your list of suspects in Ty's hit and run?"

Teagan nodded.

"Is this all you have?"

"Yes."

"Why isn't Ryan's name on here? I told you to watch out for him."

"It was, and Betty's too." Teagan admitted. "I threw them out this morning though because I don't believe they did it."

"Betty from Heavenly Bakery?"

Teagan crossed her arms. "Julian's thoughts. Not mine."

"That's an interesting theory." He laid the cards down and returned to the recliner. "I apologize for keeping you guys out of the loop. But, Paul, you understand I couldn't bring you in until I'd done some investigating on my own. I don't trust Chase Evans as far I can throw him. Teagan, I didn't believe for a minute you hurt Ty. Then, when someone broke into your house and wrote those notes in green, it confirmed it even more for me that someone was setting you up, but I had to be sure.

Evans thinks he holds all the cards in this town, but I've got my own insiders. That scoundrel thought he could shut me down and make it impossible to find any evidence. But impossible is—"

Dad joined in with Gary and they repeated their motto together.

". . . not a fact. It's an opinion. Impossible is not a declaration. It's a dare. Impossible is potential. Impossible is temporary. Impossible is nothing."

"What is that?" Aunt Connie asked.

"It's a quote from Muhammad Ali that Paul and I say to pump us up before any case that seems difficult," Gary answered. "I apologize for Detective Evans's conduct toward you the other night. Calling you Nancy Drew and an amateur sleuth was uncalled for. He's the only one on our force with such a cocky attitude."

Aunt Connie laughed. "It's okay. He may have not meant it that way, but I take it as a compliment. To be compared to my favorite childhood book hero is a dream of mine."

"That's good then, I guess." Gary cleared his throat. "I wanted to let you all know that it is believed we discovered the vehicle that hit Ty. This afternoon, Mr. Lewis checked the video from his old body shop down the street from YASO. It captured a glimpse of a yellow Mustang with damage to its fender racing out of the parking lot at the time Teagan claimed she heard Ty get hit. The driver appears to be a white male, but the individual was wearing a hat and the image is too distorted to identify the person."

"So, it has to be Pedro." Teagan blurted. "The Mustang is Pedro's car."

Aunt Connie shook her head. "Sweetie, Pedro is Hispanic. The officer said the person was white."

"Possibly white. And Pedro is fairly-light complected. Couldn't he appear white in a distorted video?"

"Maybe." Gary pursed his lips together. "Pedro, huh? He's the new chef at Marco's, correct?"

Teagan nodded.

"Why do you say the Mustang is his?" Gary questioned.

Teagan blew out a breath. "I overheard Marco say Pedro had let him borrow a yellow Mustang."

"When?"

She closed her eyes and opened them slowly.

She didn't want to throw Betty under the bus. She and Marco had hidden the car rather than call the police. "The Mustang was at Betty's yesterday, and I was spying on them."

Dad raised an eyebrow at her.

"I was just trying to see who the Mustang belonged to, and then I overheard Marco say that Pedro let him borrow it."

"That's odd because, here's a bit of information to blow your minds, the Mustang believed to have hit Ty isn't Pedro's. It belongs to the father of the dead girl in the woods. His daughter had taken it the night of the fundraiser and of course never returned home. But someone—sounds like maybe Pedro—has been driving it around town and letting people borrow it."

"So, see it's got to be Pedro?"

"Hmm." Gary tapped his forefinger against his chin several times. "I will look to see if Pedro has any connections to the girl and if he has the car hidden somewhere. I questioned your neighbors to see if they saw anything the day of your break-in. No one saw anything. Except Mr. Lewis reported that the day of the fundraiser he saw Ty was trying to pick the front door lock to your house."

Dad looked at her. "Why didn't he use the hideaway key?"

"I forgot to remind you to replace it. It wasn't there Tuesday when I got home from school."

"I used it Monday night, and I made sure I put it back."

"Who knows about the key?" Gary asked.

"Ty and Ryan."

Gary nodded. "Ryan. That makes sense."

Teagan furrowed her eyebrows. "Why? What do you have on him?"

Gary held onto the end of his chin. "I believe he's mixed up with some . . ." He tilted his head back and forth. ". . . questionable fellows. Maybe even dragged Ty in on it too. I suspect he stole the key hoping he could help himself to your house when you weren't home so he could take something he could sell."

What? That didn't make any sense. Not Ryan. "Why would he do that? You think he broke into my house? Who is he mixed up with? Pedro?"

"I'm not sure about this Pedro fellow, but Ryan's been a part of a sports gambling ring with roots out of Louisville for the last couple of months. Ryan's admitted to it. I've learned several people in Floyds Knobs are caught up in it. The most notable one being Chase Evans, himself. He has no idea he's been made."

Dad smacked his hands together once and leaned forward. "That doesn't surprise me a bit about Evans. But Ryan, man, that's a shame."

A pit formed in Teagan's stomach. How could Ryan get caught up in something like that? "I don't get why Ryan would be a part of a sports' betting ring?"

Gary shook his head. "Gambling is one of the easiest vices to fall victim too. Seems like easy money at first, but before the gambler realizes their bank accounts are drained and they are doing anything to get more money for their next gambling fix. It appears Ryan was trying to make money to pay off his deceased uncle's debts."

Ryan had been acting strange lately. Angry about money and the cruise voucher, telling Ty they had secret situations to handle, showing up late to the gala, and being rude to his mom. All out of character for him.

"He's going to lose his scholarship, right?" Teagan ran her hands down the side of her face.

"I convinced Ryan to be my inside guy. The sheriff is well-aware of this sports betting ring. He's going to do whatever he can to help Ryan keep his basketball scholarship in exchange for his cooperation."

"What about Ty? You said he might be involved too." A deep pain pulsated in her heart.

"Ryan hasn't admitted that, but I speculate Ty at least knows about Ryan's involvement, and I believe Lacey knew too."

"Why didn't Ryan or Ty tell me? They told Lacey, but not me." Teagan stood and shook her hands out.

Aunt Connie joined her. "Be glad they kept you out of it. Sounds like they were trying to protect you."

"Not too well. Someone's trying to frame me." Teagan paced. "I just can't believe all of this." She turned to Gary. "So, let me get this straight. You think someone came after Ty and kidnapped Lacey because of some sports' betting ring? Are they after Ryan?" She paused.

Gary stared forward while he shrugged and shook his head.

Her stomach dropped. For the first time, she thought maybe Ryan was guilty of hurting Ty and Lacey. No, she couldn't think like that. This was Ryan she was talking about. "Surely, you don't think Ryan is involved in Ty's hit and run and Lacey's disappearance?"

Gary stepped toward her. "I truly don't know, but he is cooperating with us every step of the way."

Teagan collapsed to her knees, the weight of all the information was too much for her to bear.

Gary rubbed her shoulder. "I'm sorry, kid." He glanced up at her dad. "Paul, I'm sorry. I should have shared this with you privately."

She looked up at Dad's partner. "No, thank you for trusting me with it. I'll be okay." She stood and smoothed her pants legs down like she'd watched her aunt do on numerous occasions. It was time to get down to business. "What do we do next?"

"You aren't doing anything." Dad said. "This isn't safe. It's not some fun little game of Clue we are playing. This is your life. I'm not risking it. I let you play along for a little while, but now you're done." He looked at his sister. "You, too."

"Uh-uh." Aunt Connie shook her head. "I don't think so, big brother. I'm going to see this through."

"I wish you wouldn't, but I know you won't listen to me. If you must, be careful."

"I always am, aren't I?"

He smirked. "I don't know about that."

"I want to help too, Daddy." Teagan hoped he could hear through her voice how much she wanted to solve this.

"I can't tell her what to do, but I can tell you." Dad pointed a stern finger in Teagan's direction.

Dad's word was final. She knew not to press the issue anymore.

Gary sat back down in the recliner. "I need everything I shared with you to stay between us. Don't tell anyone."

"I won't." Teagan's heart wrenched.

Dad and Aunt Connie nodded.

"More than just Evans is caught up in this." Gary said.

Dad looked at Teagan. "Head on to bed, kiddo."

"It's 2:00 in the afternoon."

"Take a nap. You are staying out of it."

"Come on, Dad. I'm eighteen, and I'm a suspect in all of this. Can't I at least hear the rest of what Gary has to say." She stuck out her pouty lip that got him every time. "Please, Daddy. I'm in the safety of our home with you and . . ." She batted her eyes at his partner. "Uncle Gary."

"Oh no, not the lip." He smiled. "Fine, but I mean it. You aren't to look into anything further. You let Gary do that."

She held her fingers up in the boy scout salute. "Scout's honor." Little did he know, she'd crossed her opposite fingers behind her back.

"Okay, so who else at the station is involved in the sports betting ring?" Dad asked.

"Johnny and Cory."

Dad shook his head. "Not Johnny and Cory. No."

"Yep." Gary nodded. "Ryan says they're involved."

Dad ran his hand across the top of his head. "That's terrible." He shifted on the couch. "Does Ryan have any idea where Lacey might be?"

Gary shook his head. "That's still a mystery. No signs of her at the fundraiser or after, no word to her parents, her jeep still in the driveway, just up and gone. We do have a search team alongside our best dogs, minus Colonel Mustard, of course, looking for her."

Dad tilted his neck backwards and stared at the ceiling. "I wish I could be out there with them."

"I know you do, but you need to rest that leg so it can heal, and you can get back to work soon." Gary motioned to Dad's cast.

"Earlier you mentioned the dead girl from the woods. So, from what you said about the Mustang, I presume that means you know who she is?" Dad asked.

"Yes, she's Millie Jackson, a nineteen-year-old from Louisville. Her parents have no idea what she was doing on this side of the river up here in Floyds Knobs. And there are no leads yet on a motive or who did it if she was murdered. The autopsy is still underway."

"You don't think she was murdered?" Teagan swallowed hard. "What about the note and picture of Ty found in her mouth?"

"If it wasn't for those items, the case would have been cut and dry. Considered an accident. It appears Millie had been running through the woods, fell and hit her head, then bled out."

"So, someone might have been chasing after her?" Aunt Connie questioned.

"Possibly."

Teagan covered her mouth. "Oh, my goodness. I saw her yelling at Ty and banging on his window. What if someone was after her, and she was asking for help? It wouldn't be like him to deny someone in need though. Maybe he thought she was some crazy fan and drove off. He's had to deal with a couple of those. But if she was legit in trouble or scared that would make sense why she'd run into the woods, trying to get away from whoever was after her, then she fell and hit her head."

Aunt Connie pointed a waving finger at Teagan as she spoke. "But remember Detective Evans said they'd scoped the area for hours after the gala."

"He's proven an unlikely source, though, right?" Dad suggested. "And if he had Johnny and Cory in on it, then maybe they helped cover up the girl's murder for someone but hadn't had time to dispose of the body before Teagan fell on it. Heck, maybe Evans *is* the murderer."

Aunt Connie paced the room and tapped her finger along her lips. "Or maybe Millie hid out in the woods, safe from whoever was after her while the police were in the area, but once they left, she'd had no protection and nowhere to go."

Teagan threw her hands in the air. "How about another theory? Millie was actually a crazed fan that was mad Ty blew her off, she hit him with her car. Someone saw her do it. Maybe another fan of his . . . or Lacey? Fan/Lacey went ballistic, confronted Millie, chased her off into the woods, Millie tripped and the person who caused the accident went into hiding."

Gary again nodded. "You guys are good at coming up with theories. Teagan, you sure you don't want to go into law enforcement?"

Dad shook his head. "Nope. She doesn't. She's getting a business degree where she'll be safe and sound."

Aunt Connie chuckled. "She wants to work for me, you know, and somehow I find myself caught up in quite a bit of mysteries."

"Well, you are definitely an exception to the rule, and the fact that you can't keep your nose out of other people's business doesn't help." Dad teased.

Aunt Connie stuck out her tongue.

Teagan laughed. She loved her dad and aunt. Even in the most overwhelming conversation, they'd found a way to lighten the mood.

Colonel Mustard lifted his head and cocked it to the side then went to the staircase and barked upward. He put his front paws on the second step and barked again. Seemingly satisfied, he returned to his bed.

"He's done that off and on all day." Dad shook his head.

Teagan laughed. "Colonel Mustard found a ladybug on my closet door this morning. I got rid of it, but he just won't let it go. He's silly like that sometimes."

"With the break-in the other day, he might still be on edge," Dad suggested.

"I think someone's been in the house again." Aunt Connie blurted. "Maggie's earrings are missing from Teagan's jewelry box. They were there after the break-in the other night, but now they're gone."

"Mom's earrings?" Dad looked at Teagan then Gary. "Do you think Ryan took them?"

Gary shrugged. "Maybe."

Dad looked at Teagan again. "Why didn't you say anything to me when you realized they were missing?"

"I realized it this morning. Aunt Connie and I searched for them, but just in case with everything going on I misplaced them, I didn't want to bother you with it, yet."

He looked at her. "It's not a bother. I want you to tell me everything, Teag. You didn't tell me when you hit that stop sign and now you kept the earrings from me. Is there anything else you haven't told me?"

She couldn't keep it from him any longer. She pulled the note out of her pocket. "I've been carrying this around. I found it in my room after the break-in." She handed it to Dad.

He read over it and spoke as he handed it to Gary. "Why did you keep this from us?" He looked at Aunt Connie. "Did you know about it?"

Aunt Connie shook her head and read the note over Gary's shoulder.

Teagan blew out a slow breath. "Everyone was acting like I was guilty, and this letter basically says I am. I didn't want there to be another thing to make people believe it."

Gary leaned forward. "Anything else that could help?"

She looked at Aunt Connie. "Julian and I spied on Betty yesterday. She has a green pen exactly like mine in her basement."

"Is it yours?"

"I don't know, but I think maybe. The pen is pretty rare. And Betty is dating Marco who had the yellow Mustang yesterday."

"You sure it was the same Mustang from the fundraiser?" Gary questioned.

"I think it might be. It looked similar, but there wasn't any damage to the bumper. I mean, there probably aren't too many vintage yellow Mustangs with Kentucky plates actually in the Knobs."

Gary rubbed his chin. "True. Someone could have replaced the bumper."

"How many people have those kinds of bumpers just sitting around, though?" Dad asked him.

"Good point. I'm going to head over to Ross Dole's body shop." Gary stood. "See if he's replaced a vintage Mustang bumper in the last day or two or what is the likelihood someone could have access to one fairly quickly."

The Visitor Plays a Game

Chapter Nine

Huddle Up

Teagan patted sleeping Colonel Mustard curled up on the end of her bed. Under her blankets she'd situated her pillow just so to look like her body slept underneath. Her dog's snores were as loud as a grown man's. She giggled, and then tapped her pocket for her bear mace. She tiptoed to her window, slid it and the screen up. She'd promised Dad she would stop looking into everything, but she'd also told Claire that she'd help her find Lacey. Teagan couldn't go back on her word especially after she'd made such a big deal about how sorry she was for the threats she'd made against Lacey.

Teagan considered leaving her phone so she couldn't be tracked, but that would be as stupid as those girls at the beginning of horror movies who walked into dark houses all alone. She turned off the tracker on her phone app. Her dad had access to turn it back on remotely if something really did happen to her, and she needed locating. But she was going to be fine. Julian would be with her. Besides that, she wanted to be sure she could make a phone call, text, or have access to the internet if needed.

She tossed out her emergency rope ladder and climbed out the window, then made her way to the side of the house. She attached the ladder to the gutter, shimmied down carefully, and landed on the ground. She pulled the ladder away from the gutter and hid it behind the bushes.

Now, hopefully she wouldn't get caught or run into any trouble. She hated defying her dad, but— she couldn't believe she was thinking it—Lacey Brown needed her help.

The librarian waved to Teagan as she made her way inside her home away from home. The smell of old books and lemon-vanilla hit her every time. "Evening, Mrs. Davis."

"Evening, doll. We close in thirty minutes."

"Yes, I'll be gone by then."

A female cleared her throat and Teagan turned. Aunt Connie stood next to the first bookshelf, her hands on her hips.

Uh oh. Teagan was made.

She sucked air between her teeth and wiggled her fingers at her aunt in a cautious hello. "I guess I'm in trouble."

"You think?" Aunt Connie held her phone to her ear. "Yes, she's here. I'll keep her safe. We'll meet with the girl then I'll bring her right home." She hung up. "Your dad is livid, but he agreed to let you stay."

Thank goodness. That meant he couldn't be too mad.

Out of what seemed like nowhere, Julian appeared next to Aunt Connie. "Hey, ladies." He sounded out of breath.

"You, okay?" Aunt Connie furrowed her brows.

"Yep. I just hurried to get here."

Teagan turned to the librarian. "Mrs. Davis, I

want you to meet my Aunt Connie and friend, Julian."

"Oh, this is the famous Aunt Connie."

Aunt Connie playfully pretended to flip her hair, but it was pulled back in a bun like always. "I wouldn't say famous as much as I'd say legendary."

Mrs. Davis giggled and shook her finger as she pointed at Aunt Connie. "I like her, Teagan."

Aunt Connie held her hand out. "It's nice to meet you."

"You, too. And you also, Julian."

He waved and gave a head nod.

Teagan led Aunt Connie and Julian to the back of the library where Claire had told them to meet. The place was virtually empty. One older man in a ball cap sat at the table by the car magazines, and a young mom chased her little girl in the children's room surrounded by windows decorated like a fairy garden. The shut door kept the girl's laughter from carrying into the rest of the library.

Teagan sat in a cozy, blue, Shakespearean-inspired, high-back chair. "This is my favorite spot."

"I can see why." Aunt Connie took the identical chair next to her.

Julian paced back and forth. He raked his hands through his hair and peeked at his cell phone. "It's five."

"Sit down. What's wrong?" Teagan asked.

He lowered his voice. "I can't. What if this is a trap? Ty's been hit and is in a coma, a girl's been murdered. It's not fun anymore."

Where was all of this coming from? "Was it ever fun?" Teagan asked.

"At first, I guess. It was a way to hang out with you. It felt like a game and not reality because I didn't know the players. But seeing that police car in front of my house and assuming the worse somehow opened my eyes that Ty, that girl in the woods, and Lacey are real people." He swallowed hard. "And you. What if something happens to you?" He ran his thumb down her cheek to her chin.

"She'll be fine," Aunt Connie said. "Her dad and his partner are outside in case anything happens. Okay."

Teagan glanced toward the front of the library. "They are?"

"He isn't letting you out of his sights," Aunt Connie said.

"Good." Julian let out a loud breath. "My uncle said they think they know what car hit Ty. A yellow Mustang. You were right. But they don't have any suspects yet. Couldn't tell enough from my uncle's video footage."

"I heard that too." Teagan nodded. "Have you heard anything else?"

"No." he shook his head. "You?"

Teagan looked at Aunt Connie. "No."

"It had to be Marco who hit Ty. He's lying to Betty about the Mustang, I'm sure of it. She's probably in on it too."

Teagan shook her head. Julian and his theories. "What about that Pedro guy? Marco said Pedro let him borrow it."

Julian shrugged.

But Teagan knew who the car really belonged to. If it were true that Pedro let Marco borrow it then why did Pedro have the Mustang in the first place?

"Hey, guys." Claire stepped in next to Julian.

They each greeted her.

A man in the magazine section let out several deep-in-his-chest, phlegm-producing coughs. He wiped his mouth with a handkerchief and then got up from the table and moved to the front of the library where he sat watching them.

"That man's creeping me out," Claire whispered. "Everybody does these days, though. Lacey said that Ryan has gotten involved in some pretty shady things. Ty was apparently trying to help him out."

Teagan's stomach lurched. Why did Claire and Lacey know what was going on in Ryan and Ty's lives, but she didn't?

"Lacey was scared for Ty. She tried to warn him, but he didn't listen."

"Why was she scared?" Aunt Connie asked.

"She told me Ryan had made some people mad, and if he didn't make some money quick, they were going to come after him. Lacey said Ty was going to take care of it, but I don't know any more than that."

Julian crossed his arms over his chest. "Do you have any idea who Ryan is mixed up with?"

"No." Claire shook her head.

Teagan looked at Aunt Connie. She'd keep her promise to Gary.

"Well, what do you know that can help us find

your friend?" Julian's jaw tightened.

What was his problem?

Claire stared at the floor. "I guess nothing really. The police seem to have no leads either. I told them everything I told you. I'm just hoping maybe—"

"That a couple kids and a Nancy Drew wannabe could solve this when the police can't." Julian's face turned red. "This is twisted scary stuff, and you've told us nothing that could possibly help."

Sure, they were all scared, but his attitude was uncalled for. Teagan raised her eyebrows at him. She hoped he could read between the lines that she was telling him to chill out.

Julian touched Teagan's elbow. "I'm sorry, but I'm out. My uncle already wasn't doing well today, and then that cop pulled him out on the porch to ask him questions about the video footage and the break-in at your house the other day, and now Uncle Charles is doing worse."

"He seemed okay this afternoon," Aunt Connie suggested.

"He puts on a brave face, but no he's not okay."

So, that's what was with Julian and his bad

attitude. He was worried about his uncle.

"Go ahead. Go home. Your uncle needs you." Teagan touched his arm.

"I'm sorry. I'm not normally such a jerk."

It's okay. Go. I'll call you later."

"Okay."

Julian dashed out of the library. The old man watched Julian pass, then he picked his ball cap off the table, put it on, and exited the library also.

"Your boyfriend needs an attitude adjustment? Overreact much?" Claire stuck her nose up.

"His uncle is dying."

"Oh. Sorry. Still, he didn't need to be so rude."

Aunt Connie stood. "You're right. He shouldn't have been. Thank you for meeting with us."

Claire looked down at her phone. "My mom's waiting for me in the parking lot. I told her I had to come in for a book. She doesn't let me drive anywhere alone anymore." She grabbed a book on a nearby shelf and held it up. "I do wish I knew more. I want Lacey to come home." She turned and went to the librarian's desk to check out her book and then waved before heading out the door.

"Why would Julian call me a Nancy Drew

wannabe?" Aunt Connie put her hands on her hips.

"I don't know. I've told him about how you've helped solve a crime or two before."

"Yeah, but Detective Evans called me the same thing."

Had she mentioned it to Julian? She didn't think she'd ever used that phrase. "Strange."

Aunt Connie shook her head. "Something was off about him tonight, and I think it was more than just his uncle being sick."

Chapter Ten

Hit Below the Belt

Teagan couldn't breathe. She flung her eyes open in her dark bedroom. Someone's hands over her mouth. She kicked and flailed her arms. A knee to her chest pinned her down further. Her heart raced as her limbs felt paralyzed. The moonlight faintly lit the room.

"Help!" she could barely hear her own muffled voice.

"Stop," a female whispered in her ear.

Lacey?

"I'll move my hand and get up, but you have to be quiet."

Teagan nodded.

The female removed her hands and knee. "I put

your earrings back."

"What? Lacey is that you?"

"Stay quiet!" Something hard and pointy like a gun poked her in the arm.

Teagan didn't dare speak. She swallowed hard. Where was Colonel Mustard? Why wasn't he barking?

"I couldn't take your mom's earrings."

"What?"

"Ryan told me about the earrings. He saw you wearing them at the Gala. He thought he could get a good amount of money for them."

"Why would he need money?"

"He's in trouble."

"What kind of trouble?" Teagan whispered. She knew, but she asked anyway.

"Bad trouble. Like the kind that if he doesn't cough up thousands of dollars, he's going to end up dead. His mom has already drained her bank account trying to pay back her deceased brother's debts. Now, they've come after Ryan, threatening to break his kneecaps and end his basketball career or worse. After what happened to Ty, I couldn't let them hurt Ryan too. I know the earrings wouldn't bring in the thousands he needs, but the several hundred they're worth would help buy him some time. He adores you, so he couldn't actually go through with stealing from you. The same reason he put back the cruise voucher after he took it."

So, he did take it. Teagan's body felt heavy.

"You know I don't like you, so I didn't care about taking the earrings from you. But then I heard you say they were your mom's." Lacey pushed the gun harder into Teagan's arm.

"You heard me?"

"I broke in before the sun came up this morning and snatched the earrings. I had planned to be in and out, but then your dog woke, so I hid in the back of the closet. Thank goodness for that ladybug or I would have been caught by your dog for sure. I couldn't leave then with watch dog on the case. I've had all day to contemplate what I was going to do about your mother's earrings while I waited for night and the mongrel to fall asleep. When I finally convinced myself, I could leave unnoticed with your earrings in hand, I knew I couldn't take them. I remember how hard it was on you when your mom died."

Teagan nodded, her heart racing. "You were my best friend back then."

"Yeah, well things change." Lacey's voice softened as she lowered the gun and climbed off the bed. "You know my mom died last year. The cancer finally took her, and if someone stole something of hers that she'd given me, I'd be devastated. I couldn't do that to you, whether I like you or not."

"Yeah, I get it, so why all the theatrics with the gun and waking me up." Teagan sat up in the bed. "Why not put them back and sneak out? I'd never be the wiser."

"I don't know. I guess I thought I owed you an apology . . . for everything." Lacey pointed the gun back at Teagan. "Now shut up."

Teagan slipped her legs over the edge of the bed. "I want to help you if you'll put the gun down."

Lacey dropped the gun to her side. "It's not even loaded."

That was a relief. She stood and picked up a sweater from her chair, wrapping it around her. "What can I do to help?"

The girl shrugged. "Nothing. There is nothing anyone can do. I was doomed the second Ty told me what was going on."

Teagan wanted to throw up. "I don't understand. How could he and Ryan get mixed up in all this? And why did they tell you and not me?"

Lacey huffed. "I'm Ty's girlfriend."

Teagan put her hands on her hips. "And I'm both of their best friend." The words stung coming out. Maybe Teagan wasn't as close to them as she thought. Were they going to walk out of her life like Lacey had done when Teagan had needed her most?

"Well, they trusted me and not you."

Teagan sat on the edge of her bed. "Why? None of this makes sense. None of it."

"Ryan's trying to pay back the debt from his uncle's gambling problem." Lacey spoke in a gentle tone again. "He only got tangled up in it when he found out someone had been threatening his mom after her brother's death. Ty was trying to help Ryan get out. But they took care of Ty, didn't they? Ran him over. Proof that once you are in, you can't get out. Now, people are after me too. These people are powerful, Teagan. Their boss is smart. Mean."

Teagan's heart dropped to her stomach. "Who's their leader?"

"Nobody knows."

"Oh, my goodness, Lacey. I had no idea that Ryan has been caught up in something like this."

Lacey took in a deep breath. "He didn't want you to know."

"Why?"

Lacey sneered. "He didn't want to disappoint the great Teagan Wright."

What was that supposed to mean? Why was Lacey always such a jerk? "So, why did they tell you about it? Ty not care enough to keep you safe?"

Lacey sneered. "No. I knew something was going on and I pestered Ty until he relented and told me." She sounded proud of herself.

"That doesn't surprise me."

"What's that supposed to mean?"

Teagan's stomach knotted. "You only care about yourself."

"How do you figure?"

Teagan had needed to have this conversation for way too long. "After my mom died, you abandoned me."

"Me? Abandon you? I don't think so. You retreated from me when I needed you. Your mom died and my mom found out she had cancer. Everyone felt sorry for poor pitiful Teagan, and no one cared I was terrified I was going to lose my mom too. Right or wrong I was ten years old, and I was jealous of you." She scraped a tear off her cheek.

"Jealous of my mom dying?" Teagan could hardly believe what she was hearing.

Lacey stared at the floor like a balloon losing all its air. "Of the attention."

Pain welled up in her chest. "I didn't want any of it. I wanted my mom." Teagan raised her voice.

"I understand that now. I'm sorry for all of it." Lacey swiped at another tear, but they kept coming. She glanced up at Teagan. "Forgive me?"

Who was this person in front of her? A broken, hurting girl. A girl without a mama. Teagan knew how that felt all too well.

"I've missed you." The words had left Teagan's lips before she realized it.

"I've missed you too."

Teagan took a deep breath as Lacey stuffed the empty weapon in her waistband under her tee shirt. Everything was out, but there were more pressing questions that needed answered. "Everyone is worried about you. Where have you been?"

"I found out that Detective Evans who lives down the street from me is big in the gambling scene." Lacey bowed her head. "It was stupid, but I really thought I could solve Ryan's problem. Ty and Ryan both told me not to, but when do I listen to what anyone tells me to do?"

"You are pretty thick headed." Teagan couldn't resist the jab.

"Thanks."

"You're welcome."

She went on, "Anyway, I went to the detective's house the afternoon of the gala and tried to blackmail him into giving me three thousand dollars in exchange for not telling his wife or the chief what he'd been up to. It backfired, and he drew his gun on me, but I sprayed him with my mace. He told me I was dead if he ever found me. I made it to Ryan's house on foot. His mom snuck me in the YASO basement, and I've been hiding there ever since."

Teagan remembered the laundry basket full of blankets and pillows and the bag full of food she'd tried to help Mrs. Dodger with the night of the fundraiser. It was all for Lacey.

"Does you dad know you're safe?"

Lacey shook her head. "It's better he doesn't."

"But he has to be beside himself with worry."

"He can't know." Anger flashed in her eyes. "They'll come after him too. The boss's goons threatened Ryan again that if he didn't at least bring them $500 by tomorrow they'd not only break his legs but hurt his mom. So, ta-da, that's why I'm here. I couldn't let anyone else get hurt." Lacey wrung her fingers as her voice broke. She bowed her head and practically crumpled before Teagan's eyes. "Oh, my goodness, what if Ty isn't okay?" Her voice lowered to a whisper. "I love him so much." She glanced up at Teagan again, showing mascara streaks down her cheeks. "Is he okay?"

"I don't know. Ms. Jones won't let me see him. She thinks I did it. The police do too." And there wasn't a thing she could do about it. "They even think I have something to do with your disappearance."

"Really? Now that's crazy. You still can't hurt a spider, can you?"

Teagan shook her head. "That's what I said." She didn't know why, but it comforted her that

Lacey still remembered something about her.

Lacey gave an almost silent laugh then abruptly stopped. "What am I going to do? I'm dead if Detective Evans find me."

Teagan made her way to Lacey and put a hand on her shoulder. "I need to talk to my dad. He'll know what to do."

Lacey's forehead scrunched together making lines between her eyebrows. She shook her head a few times then blew out a deep breath. "Okay."

Teagan ran down the hallway and tapped on Dad's bedroom door. "Daddy."

Still no peep from Colonel Mustard. He had to be out cold somewhere. Probably collapsed after sensing Lacey in the closet all day.

Dad stuck his head out. She quickly explained to him what was going on. They rushed down the hallway to her room.

Lacey was gone. With the window open, the curtains flapped against the breeze.

This was too much. Teagan followed closely behind her father as he hobbled down the stairs, gun in hand. Where had Lacey gone? Had she darted off into the night or had something more sinister happened?

Please no.

"If Lacey's not down here or in our house still, she couldn't have gotten far." Dad waved his pointer finger in a circular motion in the air. "Gary's on patrol tonight along with several other good cops, They'll find her. Stay close behind me."

He crept into the kitchen and flipped on the light.

The back door stood wide open, unattended. The cool, middle-of-the-night air brought a chill down Teagan's back. Why was it open? Had Lacey gone out the back door instead of the window, but that wasn't possible. She would have passed Teagan in the hallway.

"Colonel!" Teagan shouted and dashed into the living room. "Colonel. Where are you boy?"

"What's wrong." Aunt Connie, in a red bathrobe, met her at the bottom of the steps.

"Lacey was here. Gun. My mom's earrings.

Detective Evans. Gambling." Teagan tried to catch her breath to explain, but the words wouldn't come out until she blurted. "I can't find Colonel Mustard and the back door's wide open."

Dad hobbled into the entry hall. "I'm sure I locked it after dinner. Colonel?" He whistled. "Here, boy."

Teagan ducked back inside the kitchen. She grabbed a flashlight from the cabinet above the sink and called out again. "Colonel."

Dad's voice echoed through the house as Teagan threw the light over the back lawn and toward the hedges.

"He's nowhere in the house." Aunt Connie joined her on the patio.

She caught the gate in the beam. "Oh, no." It hung open. She wrapped her arm around her chest and ran down the driveway. "Colonel! Colonel! Colonel!" When she reached the sidewalk, she looked both ways. "Colonel! Colonel!"

"Could you keep it down? It's late." Mr. Lewis grumbled from the porch swing. He sat slouched with his arms across his chest.

Her heart hammered hard against her chest. She

Shawna Robison Young

turned slowly, spying her aunt coming down the driveway.

Dad shuffled out of the front door on his crutches. "Sorry, our dog got out." He waved to Mr. Lewis. "He's never run off before."

"I know a little bit about dogs." Mr. Lewis stood and made his way to the railing of his porch. "If you don't mind some advice from an old man."

"Sure." Dad nodded.

"Your German Shepherd, Colonel, is it?"

Dad nodded again. Teagan's heart was still pumping in overdrive from Lacey's visit and now her missing dog. Why was her dad wasting time talking to him? They didn't need him. Dad was a top K9 handler who'd trained Colonel Mustard and many more over the years.

"If he's a good dog, he'll wander back." Mr. Lewis cleared his throat. "Excuse me." He wiped his mouth with the back of his hand. "If the dog's mischievous, he'll give you quite a chase." He held onto the top of the rail while he stared at them. "God help your dog though if he finds his way into my yard."

"What? What are you going to do to my dog?

207

Kill him?" Teagan blurted.

"Teagan." Dad gave her stern eyes and shook his head.

Mr. Lewis' laughter held the deep sound of phlegm in his chest. "I don't hurt animals. So don't you worry your pretty little head. Your dog won't be the one to pay for his trespassing."

Was he challenging her? He might be the type that gave threats and orders and people jumped but not her. He'd be sorry if he even looked at Colonel Mustard funny.

"Sir." Aunt Connie cleared her throat. "Surely, you aren't provoking a teenage girl who's upset about her missing dog."

Mr. Lewis stared at them as he walked to his door and tapped against it.

Dad stood tall. "If you know what's good for you, sir, you won't say another word."

"Is that so?" Mr. Lewis cracked his screen door. Growling, Killer stuck his nose out and barred teeth between the small opening.

Dad turned his back on Mr. Lewis. "Don't worry about him. He's all talk."

"For a sick man, he's awful feisty," Aunt

Connie whispered.

Dad shook his head and widened his eyes. "All talk. We'll find Colonel. Ignore him."

After two hours of searching, calling, and driving around town, Teagan conceded in silence that her dog was indeed missing. Without discussing it with her or Aunt Connie, Dad turned toward home in his police car. The night sky was still hanging on as the orange sun started to rise. The pink, blue, and black layered on top of each other, but she couldn't enjoy it. Too much heaviness on her heart.

Colonel Mustard was nowhere to be found. Hopefully, Mr. Lewis was right, and he'd return. Which one of them had left the door and gate open? She hated to admit it, but none of them were the type to do that. Dad was always a stickler about keeping the doors closed and locked. And she would never leave a door wide open or forget to shut a gate. As for Aunt Connie, she hadn't even been out in the back that day.

Could someone have taken her dog? She'd never consider such a thing normally, but with the break ins and Lacey's assault on her, she couldn't ignore the possibility.

But why? Was it a warning? She couldn't allow herself to think what illegal gamblers would do to Colonel Mustard.

Dad rounded the corner to their street. The sunrise was even more beautiful now, the sky brilliant shades of pink, red, orange, yellow, and blue with the very top of the sky black, keeping the street dark. As they neared Mr. Lewis's house, his garage door was going down. Teagan caught sight of the bottom of a yellow Mustang. She took a second look, but the door had already closed all the way.

Lacey's words echoed in her mind, "These people are powerful, Teagan. Their boss is smart. Mean."

Mean.

The Mustang confirmed it. Mr. Lewis was the boss, and he'd attempted to lead the police off his tail by coming forward with evidence. Had he killed the girl in the woods, stolen her car, and then ran over Ty, or had he made someone else do it? He was just mean enough. There was no telling what the man was capable of.

From across the room, Teagan's cell phone rang. She darted out of bed and ran to it. What if it was someone with information about Colonel? The bright sun hit her in the eyes through the slat. What time was it?

She grabbed her phone.

"Hello."

"Hello, dear." The voice sounded kind. Betty? "I heard about Colonel Mustard. Anything yet?"

"No." Teagan looked to her alarm clock: 10:15 a.m. Church started in fifteen minutes. She guessed they were skipping today.

"I'm sorry to hear that. Your dad stopped by this morning with posters. He put them in every shop. This town will rally together and find Colonel Mustard. What would the Christmas parade be without the town's favorite German shepherd in a

Santa hat sitting in the passenger seat of your dad's cruiser? Or the police dog skills show at Harvest Homecoming? Or the obedient way he sits outside my bakery waiting for you to return and for me to give him a dog cookie."

Dad probably hadn't gone back to sleep after he called Gary and told him about the Mustang in Mr. Lewis's garage. All the while Teagan had sawed logs without a care in the world. That wasn't true. She'd tossed and turned for hours, consumed with thoughts about Ryan, his mom, Ty, Lacey, Mr. Lewis, and Colonel Mustard until finally dozing.

"Would you stop by this afternoon, dear? I have something for you." Betty said from the other end of the line.

"Sure. I'll be over shortly."

Teagan had to check on Ryan. She called his number, but it went straight to voicemail. "Call me. Are you okay? I'm worried." Next, she called Mrs. Dodger, but again straight to voicemail. "Would you or Ryan please call me."

They had to be okay. She couldn't handle much more.

She brushed her hair and pulled it up in a

ponytail and then threw on her glasses. She looked down at her leggings and the tee shirt she'd put on after her shower the night before. Nice enough. She went to the bathroom, brushed her teeth, and then went downstairs.

Aunt Connie leaned over the counter with her nose in a book. An opening door with the title *Wrong Way Out* decorated the cover. Nice that her aunt could shed the tension from last night so easily. She seemed oblivious to Teagan's entrance. "Is it good?"

Her aunt actually flinched and looked up at her, drawing in a deep breath. "Oh, yes. Riveting adventure about the end times."

A snore emanated from the recliner. Dad had the remote in his hand, but his eyes were shut.

Aunt Connie lowered her voice. "We were out all morning, posting reward signs, and searching again."

Teagan frowned. "I don't think we're going to find him. Mr. Lewis had someone take him. I know it."

Aunt Connie's face softened. "You know your dad said not to jump to conclusions. We need more proof."

"I know it's him. I know it. The Mustang is in his garage."

"Gary said it's not there and Mr. Lewis acted like he knew nothing about it."

"Oh, because Mr. Lewis is a reliable source."

"I wonder if your eyes were playing tricks on you." Aunt Connie tucked a strand of hair behind Teagan's ear. "If you're right about Mr. Lewis, then do you think Julian knows? Seeing as how he has a sixth-sense about people."

"I don't know. I don't think so, but what do I know? I didn't even know Ryan and Ty were in trouble." She wrung her fingers. "Has there been any word on Lacey? I hope she's okay and just ran off scared last night."

"Your dad said that according to Gary, the departments upped the search for Lacey through Kentucky, Ohio, and Illinois. Now that the police know she's alive and in danger, she is top priority. Gary told your dad there is no sign that Lacey was ever at the YASO building, and Ryan and his mom appear to have skipped town, so maybe all three are together. Let's hope they're safe."

Chapter Eleven

Not Even Bits O' Brickle can Fix It

"Colonel!" Teagan called his name one more time before she and Aunt Connie stepped up to Heavenly Bakery. Aunt Connie hadn't allowed her to come alone. Sometimes her aunt could be bossy, but Teagan understood why she shouldn't be alone.

The poster of Colonel Mustard hung on the bakery door right at her eye level, a picture of him sitting in front of their fireplace last year. *German Shepherd. Male. Colonel Mustard. Reward. $500.*

She sniffed up a tear. He had to come home. He was her buddy. Her comforter. The one who'd helped heal her ten-year-old broken heart after the loss of her mother. She turned and shouted his name again and looked around.

Betty opened the door. "Good morning." She invited them inside. "You all want a donut?"

"Please." Betty's donut wouldn't bring Colonel Mustard back, but it sure would satisfy her grumbly stomach. Teagan looked at Aunt Connie. "They are heavenly, of course."

Betty laughed. "I never get tired of hearing you say that."

"A donut sounds lovely."

"What kind can I get you ladies?" Betty went behind the counter and placed her hands on top of the display case.

Teagan looked inside and pointed. "That one with the cherries on top."

"Great choice. It will take your breath away it's so yummy!" Betty removed it and handed it to Teagan. "And you?" She looked at Aunt Connie.

"Hmm." Aunt Connie tapped her cheek. "Do I want to be plain and boring or adventurous?"

"I'm always up for a tastebud adventure." Betty giggled.

While Aunt Connie looked over the selection, Teagan took her donut to a table by the window and looked outside. Her once perfect town was now jaded and corrupt by Mr. Lewis who runs people over, murders girls, and threatens mothers and teenage kids. She shuddered.

"Oh, yes, the snickerdoodle crumble donut." Betty sang. "It's to die for."

To die for? Maybe her aunt ought not to have that one.

Betty handed the donut to Aunt Connie, and the two of them joined Teagan. Betty put her hands on the table. "I asked you here because I need to apologize." She got up from the table and grabbed a cardboard box and then returned. "I made you a new batch of Heavenly Bits O' Brickle."

"No, I'm sorry I went down in your basement the other day. I truly was trying to get Julian to come back upstairs," Teagan explained.

Betty patted Teagan's hand. "I know you would never invade my privacy. It's just that I've had several kids go down there lately. For one, it's a health hazard for them to be in my kitchen. For another, I wouldn't go into their homes uninvited so why would they do that to mine?"

"I'm sorry."

"I know you are, dear." She handed the box of

cookies to Teagan. A diamond ring flashed on Betty's left ring finger.

"Oh, what's that. I just knew you had a new boyfriend. I didn't know it was serious."

Betty grinned from ear to ear. "It's all happened so fast, but I'm happy. Happier than I've been in years."

Teagan held Betty's hand as she admired the ring. "I see that."

"Who's the lucky guy," Aunt Connie asked.

"Marco Ricci."

"Marco as in the man with the fantastic Italian Restaurant?" She clasped her hands together and smiled her broad smile.

Betty put her hands to her heart. "Yes."

"Congratulations." Aunt Connie took a bite of her donut.

Teagan couldn't bring herself to say it. She was happy for Betty, sure, but she was afraid Marco might be caught up in all of it. After all, he did have the yellow Mustang the other day. The Mustang that had been in Mr. Lewis's garage. The dead girl's car.

"I know you just forgave me for being down in your basement, but I have to admit something else."

Teagan wrung her fingers under the table.

Betty widened her eyes.

"Please don't be mad at me, but I saw the yellow Mustang in your parking lot the other day. I heard Marco say it's Pedro's. I have to know, did Marco talk to Pedro about the Mustang? It wasn't Pedro's car like he told Marco. It belonged to the girl found in the woods." Teagan's voice sounded shaky as she spoke.

Betty put her hand on her heart. "I'm not mad. I promise. We've talked with Pedro and the police about it already. Pedro was looking to buy the Mustang from the girl's family. They were friends. Apparently, her ex-boyfriend is roommates with Pedro. She was going to stay with them for a few days while she let him test drive it, but she never showed up at the apartment. The Mustang, however, was in his apartment's garage with the fender already bent in. Pedro assumed Millie had decided not to stay. He was glad because, apparently, she and the ex-boyfriend had a volatile relationship."

"But the Mustang wasn't dented in when you had it."

"Yes. Pedro wanted to impress Marco by letting

him borrow it, so he had it fixed. His roommate knows someone who has lots of old vintage car parts lying around."

"Who's his roommate?"

Betty shrugged. "I don't know."

"So, is the roommate a suspect in the girl's death? Ty's hit and run? Do you think Pedro knows and he's covering up for his roommate?"

"I told you all I know." At least she didn't look upset with her for her spying.

So how did Mr. Lewis end up with the car? She knew she'd seen it. And who'd had the Mustang the night of the break-in at her house? Was it Pedro? The roommate?

Teagan searched out the window, hoping Colonel Mustard would walk by as if he'd been out for a night stroll and was returning home. But no dog. Two older men sat on the bus stop bench, a couple kissed by the fountain in front of Marco's Italian Bistro, a few police officers stood beside a parked cruiser, and Julian talked on his cell phone while he paced in front of the pharmacy.

He pointed and shook his head as he spoke. Did he know what his uncle was up to? She had to know.

"I'll be right back." Teagan darted out the door. She made her way across the street to him.

"This has gotten way out of hand. You better take care of it." He pulled his phone away from his ear and pushed his finger hard against it. He turned around and jerked when he saw her. The stern look in his eyes softened when he saw her. "Hey."

"You, okay?"

"Yeah. I'm fighting with the insurance, doctor's office, and the pharmacy to get Uncle Charles's medicine. Sorry, you had to see me like that. I'm stressed."

"I'm sorry to hear that." Her stomach tightened. Should she ask him about the Mustang? Was it the appropriate time? He'd been dealing with so much already with his uncle's health. How should she approach her question? "Is your uncle involved in any shady business practices?"

Julian scrunched his nose. "Like what? He's a crotchety old man, but he ran an honest mechanic shop his whole career until he retired a while back. Now he just uses his old shop to store all his vehicles. Where is all this coming from?"

How did she ask without just coming out and

saying it? "I don't know how else to say it, but I saw the yellow Mustang in your uncle's garage."

He scrunched his nose again. "The one down here? His old body shop? Were you spying on him?"

"No. It was nothing like that. It was the garage at his house."

"That's odd. How did you see it? His garage is always closed."

"Colonel Mustard got out last night, and we were out looking for him in the middle of the night."

"Oh, man. I'm sorry. Did you find him?"

"No."

"That's a bummer. I'll keep my eyes out for him."

"Thank you, but anyway, when we came back home your uncle's garage door was shutting, and I saw it."

Julian looked down at his phone. "That doesn't make any sense. He has a yellow Corvette. Perhaps that's what you saw? When he can't sleep, he takes his cars out for a spin." He grunted. "I can't believe you are accusing my uncle. When you wrote his name down on your little cards, I played along, but I knew he had nothing to do with your friend's accident."

"Accident? It was no accident. Someone hit Ty on purpose and drove off."

"How do you know it was on purpose?"

She put her hands on her hips. "I just do."

"I'm done playing this game with you, little girl. You are accusing innocent people."

Little girl? Sure, he was older than her, but that didn't seem to bother him all the times he tried to put the charm on as if he liked her.

"Didn't you do the same with Ryan and Betty? I know they aren't guilty, but you just keep pushing their and Marco's names on me."

"None of them is a dying old man. And everyone keeps telling you Ryan is the one mixed up in shady things. Betty's the one with your pen in her basement. Marco is the one we saw with the Mustang."

"Pedro's Mustang." She stood her ground.

"Oh, I thought it was my uncle's Mustang." Julian stepped in close.

"Look. I don't think it's your uncle's or Pedro's Mustang." Of course, Teagan had known that yesterday when Gary had told her it belonged to the dead girl in the woods and Betty had just confirmed it. She'd promised Gary she wouldn't tell anyone, and she wouldn't break her word.

"So, whose is it then? Mine? You going to accuse me next?"

"Of course not."

"But you claim the Mustang is in Uncle Charles's garage. Maybe I put it there. I mean, you think you are so smart and know everything. Apparently, a murderer has been right under your nose all along, and you didn't have a clue."

She glared at him. "Stop it."

"Hey, you're Paul's girl, right?" One of the police officers standing by his car yelled across the street.

"Yes, sir."

"You all right?" the man asked.

"Yes, thank you. We are just talking."

The police officer nodded and turned back to his conversation with the other cop.

Julian's eyes softened. Maybe the police officer had brought him back to reality. "Look. My uncle doesn't have a yellow Mustang. He's all bark and no bite, okay. You must have seen his Corvette. I don't have time to do this. I have to get his medications and get back to him." He turned and went into the pharmacy before she had time to say another word.

She felt more confused now than ever. Maybe Julian was right, and she hadn't seen a Mustang.

She returned to the bakery as Betty and Aunt Connie came out the front door.

Aunt Connie motioned for Teagan to join them in the parking lot. "We're going to walk down to the YASO building with Betty. She left her cake tier holders in the kitchen. She's baking a cake this week for a big wedding. You have keys to the building, right?"

"If we are hiking it, I'm going to go in to grab a water bottle really quick," Betty said. "You ladies want me to grab you one too?"

"Sure," Aunt Connie replied and then gave Teagan a worried, questioning look as Betty ran inside. "You okay to go back to the YASO?"

Teagan shrugged. "I could just give her the keys and we could go back home. She's had the key hundreds of times to set up for various events." Teagan wanted to get back home and see if Dad had gotten any news on Colonel Mustard or Lacey and the others. He probably would have called her, though, if he'd heard anything.

Aunt Connie whispered, "I want to get in the building too and look around to see if that's where Mrs. Dodger hid Lacey. Maybe we can find some clues as to where she's at now. But we do need to be cautious. I believe you that Betty isn't involved and her story about the Mustang seems like it could be true, but she did have a green pen exactly like yours, so stay close to me, okay?"

"Okay." Teagan hated not trusting Betty, but Aunt Connie was right.

Teagan walked behind Aunt Connie and Betty. They chatted like old friends, but Teagan couldn't drag herself out of the funk that settled on her heart. The YASO building was closed on Sundays, so there were no cars in the parking lot.

Teagan pulled her keys out and gripped them. She unlocked the door and turned off the alarm on the wall right inside. She flipped on the lights next to the alarm. Even though the skylight and windows lit the entryway, further down the hallway would be dark.

Cool air rushed over Teagan and sent a chill down her spine. She shivered.

"You okay, dear?" Betty asked.

"Yes." Teagan touched her beltloop for her mace and then pulled back on the door to be sure it had caught and was locked.

Betty made her way down the hallway. Teagan and Aunt Connie followed. When setting up for the fundraiser Teagan had enjoyed the silence, but now she longed to hear a basketball dribbling, sneakers squeaking on the court, coaches training the athletes, kids encouraging one another.

She peered at her phone: 11:30 a.m. The building would open at two. Who opened it? Ty did from time to time now that he was one of the coaches.

Thoughts of Ty weighed down her heart further. Would he ever wake up? Prove to his mom that Teagan had nothing to do with his hit and run.

She'd give Ty an earful, of course, for not telling her what was going on. She got it though, she guessed. Dad was a cop, but he would have helped them. He wouldn't have been happy with them, but he would have helped.

Betty pushed open the door to the kitchen and flipped on the lights. Then she screamed. In the corner, Ryan sat slouched with his head leaning forward into his chest. Teagan's heart accelerated. His face was swollen and covered in blood and bruises.

She ran to him. "Ryan. Ryan." She shook his shoulders. Nothing. She put her two fingers to his neck. She couldn't find a pulse, but she didn't give up. She was never good at finding pulses. "Help." She looked at Aunt Connie. Her aunt crashed to her knees onto the floor next to Teagan and began feeling around for a pulse.

"Call 9-1-1!" Teagan shouted to Betty who still stood in the doorway frozen and staring forward.

Betty blinked a few times as she pulled her phone from her purse. She pushed the numbers and put the phone to her ear. "Yes, Betty Adams. I'm at the YASO building on Paoli Pike. There's a boy here who appears to have been beaten up."

Aunt Connie shouted. "I found it. He's got a

pulse." She leaned her head near his mouth. "And he's breathing."

"Thank goodness."

"They're on the way." Betty put her phone in her purse.

Teagan stood and looked at Betty. "You stay here with Ryan. Aunt Connie, come with me."

Before either one could respond, Teagan ran out the side door into the gym and flipped all the lights on.

"What are you doing?" Aunt Connie asked.

"Looking for Mrs. Dodger and Lacey. Just because they weren't here earlier doesn't mean someone didn't bring them back." Teagan scanned the gym and then sprinted to the stage and backstage. She tripped over a curtain and slammed against the floor. She picked herself up and shook the pain in her wrist away. "They aren't back here."

Teagan ran out of the gym to Mrs. Dodger's office. Locked. She pulled out her keys and unlocked it. No sign of Mrs. Dodger, but her office chair had been flipped, papers flung around the room, and drips of blood sprinkled across her desk.

Outside sirens blared.

"I'll let them in." Aunt Connie ran out of the room.

Teagan pulled out her phone and dialed Gary's number. The sirens outside stopped. The other phone line rang twice, and then he answered.

"Hey Teagan, what's up?"

"I'm at the YA—"

From behind her someone took her phone. "You aren't calling anyone," a man said.

She reached for her mace as he put his gloved hand over her mouth and his other arm around her body, restraining her arms. She wiggled back and forth and tried biting him, but she couldn't get hold of any skin. She stomped on his foot, but he swept her feet out from underneath her, and she crashed to the floor. Without letting go, he fell on top of her. Pain shot through the wrist she'd already fallen on.

She let out a muffled scream.

"Shut up," he yelled in her ear.

She turned her head, trying for a look of him, but he butted the side of her head with his chin.

Where was Aunt Connie? Betty? Had the paramedics even come into the building? Were they helping Ryan while this psycho was after her?

She glanced at his shoulder. Dark blue shirt. Police? Or could be EMT.

"Let's go." The voice came from behind them.

Teagan's captor let go of her. She flipped over. Detective Evans. He hit her upside the head with his elbow.

The Visitor Plays a Game

Chapter Twelve

There's No "I" in Team

Teagan fluttered her eyes open. Her head hammered. Her mouth was taped, and her feet and hands bound. Someone was carrying her down a flight of stairs. She forced her eyes open. She looked side to side. It was too dark to see anything. Where was Aunt Connie?

"Put them in there," a man demanded. "He wants them alive, so he can see the look on their faces when he reveals himself before he disposes of them. I told you he's a sick one."

Something screeched across the floor and a tiny light lit the space around it. The man shouting the orders held the door open as the person holding her threw her into a dark room. Was that Officer Cory at the door and Officer Johnny who'd thrown her in the room? It was hard to tell in the dark. Gary had said they were involved. What did they want with her?

"Johnny? Cory?" Teagan could barely get their names out.

"I thought you said they were out cold. Now she's recognized us." Cory took a step forward.

"Not to worry. Boss said he'd take care of her personally."

Boss? Of course. Detective Evans. He was just cocky enough to want to show his face before killing them. Another elbow came down onto her face.

Teagan woke to the sounds of footsteps above her and the low murmuring of voices around her, but she couldn't see anything in the pitch black. A musty smell burned her nose, and water dripped from somewhere. Her body lay sideways, her hands and feet still bound, but her mouth free of the tape.

"Hello." Teagan slid herself into a seated

position.

"Shh, sweetie," Aunt Connie whispered from somewhere in the room. "I don't want them to hear we took the tape off our mouths."

"We?" Teagan kept her voice low.

Bound fingers touched hers as her aunt spoke from a different spot in the room. "Ryan, Mrs. Dodger, Betty, and Lacey."

So, who was touching her? Teagan looked to the side, but as if deep in the middle of a cave, not even a trace of light filtered in. "Who is this?" she wiggled her fingers against the other person.

"Lacey," she croaked out.

Teagan did her best to squeeze Lacey's fingers. Thank goodness she was okay. Well, if this was being okay. At least, she wasn't dead.

"Where are we?" Teagan whispered.

"My basement." Betty gasped. "I guess it's going to be true soon enough that there are dead bodies down here." She wept.

"Stop," Aunt Connie bossed. "We are going to figure this out together."

Footsteps pounded against the stairs and loud voices boomed.

"Lay down toward my hands," Lacey whispered.

Teagan obeyed, and Lacey moved tape against Teagan's mouth. "Now do mine."

Lacey laid down and Teagan shifted around feeling for Lacey's mouth. She found it and smoothed the tape over Lacey.

The voices sounded like they were right outside of the room. Teagan clutched her fists together.

The shelf screeched against the floor and the door opened. A flashlight shined across the room, and Teagan closed her eyes at first against the brightness, but they soon adjusted. She squinted to see, her glasses obviously missing from her face. Aunt Connie had blood trickling down her forehead, Mrs. Dodger looked unharmed, but Ryan lay limp on the ground, the same as in the kitchen of the YASO building. Teagan peeked at Lacey. Her face swollen, the outside of her clothes covered in blood.

Teagan tried seeing the person holding the flashlight, but between her blurry vision and the blinding light, it was impossible.

Nothing is impossible, Dad's voice rang in her ears. She repeated the words in her head from

Muhammad Ali he'd quoted every time she doubted herself. *Impossible is not a fact. It's an opinion. Impossible is not a declaration. It's a dare. Impossible is potential. Impossible is temporary. Impossible is nothing.*

She closed her eyelids shut and then forced them open against the light. She squinted, getting her blurry eyes to focus. Cory moved the flashlight to the side and turned to listen to a voice outside of the room.

"Hey boss," Johnny said outside the door.

Detective Evans walked inside the room and shined a flashlight in front of his face while pointing a gun toward Aunt Connie. "Take a real good look at this mug because it's the last time, you'll see it."

Teagan's heart tore through her chest. This couldn't be the end.

"Boss. He said to wait." Cory entered the room.

"You think I take orders from him? He's a pansy. Can't even do his own dirty work. Accidently killed that ex-girlfriend of his, left her in the woods, and made us take care of it."

He had to be talking about Pedro's roommate.

Detective Evans continued, "You think he's

gonna do anything about this situation?" He pointed toward them with his head. "He's just a scared little kid playing grown-up."

"What'd you call me?" Julian entered the room pointing a gun at Detective Evans. "I took care of the boy, didn't I?"

Boy? What boy? What was he talking about? What was Julian doing here? Had he come to rescue them?

Detective Evans swung around. "I called you a scared little kid. You didn't take care of nothin'. Just made a mess of things up here in the Knobs. Go back to your side of the river. Yucky Kentucky. I've got things taken care of here now. There's a new boss in town."

"I don't think so." Julian fired his gun at Detective Evans.

Teagan screamed under the tape across her mouth. What was he doing?

The detective's gun slipped from his hand as he fell to the ground and clutched his leg. Julian kicked the man's gun away from him and picked it up while keeping his pointed at Officers Cory and Johnny who'd drawn their guns from their holsters and pointed them at Julian.

Everything was happening so fast.

Julian shook his head. "Why don't you put those away, boys." He held a gun in each hand. "Fun fact about me. I'm ambidextrous and a sharpshooter in both hands. National Champion three years in a row. I could take this whole room out in less than a minute."

"He's all talk." Detective Evans attempted to stand but fell back to the ground, blood gushing from his leg. "Julian couldn't run the Jones boy down effectively or shoot to kill me. I'm telling you just a scared boy."

What? Julian hit Ty? This made no sense. He was a nice guy, right? Took care of his ailing uncle, brought dinners, cookies, and flowers. He couldn't have been the one who ran Ty over.

Julian laughed. "Who's to say I didn't strike you right where I meant to? Can you get up? No, right?" He clicked his tongue. "I like to instill fear." He shot at the ground next to Cory and Johnny. "Put the guns down and kick them toward me or next time I won't miss your feet, and for fun and target practice I'll shoot that sweet little baker right in her heavenly heart."

Betty mumbled and moaned under the tape as she violently shook her head and scooted backward. Why was Julian acting this way?

The officers laid their guns down.

Detective Evans groaned. "What a bunch of cream puffs. He isn't capable of killing anyone."

Julian kicked the guns the rest of the way out the door behind him. "Truly, I'm not in the killing business. I'm in the making people do what I say business." He leaned into the detective's face. "I sure convinced you and your goons to do my heavy lifting." He stood and gestured with his palm upward. "Killing, if you will, and other various tasks that I don't care to get my hands dirty doing."

Officer Johnny moved toward the guns at the door.

Julian pointed his at him. "I wouldn't do that if I were you."

Johnny rushed to the door anyway, and Julian shot him in the back. The officer crashed to the ground, face first.

"I don't like having to do that." Julian shook his head and paced in front of the door, stepping over

Johnny. "Killing my ex-girlfriend was an accident. She shouldn't have run from me. I loved Millie. I wouldn't have hurt her. But she thought she could take me down. Tried to convince your buddy, Ty, to help her." He looked at Teagan. "He knew too much between what my ex and Ryan had told him. Ty needed to be warned."

Teagan finally understood. Julian was Pedro's roommate. He was the ex-boyfriend of the girl from the woods. Julian had done it all. Not Mr. Lewis. She wiggled, trying to get free of the ropes and tape. She wanted to shout and tell him he was sick and a liar.

He stepped toward her and ran a gun along the side of her face. He looked at Evans. "Thanks for the tip about Teagan's relationship with Ty and her green pen so we could frame her for everything. It was genius, I must admit. And a lot of fun."

She fought against the ropes again. What did Julian want? Why had he brought them all here? Why hadn't he killed them already? She should have listened to her original instincts about him, but no she'd gotten caught up in his web of deceit and charm. Dumb. She was smarter than that.

He yanked the tape from her mouth. "You have something to say."

"What's wrong with you?"

He raised his cheek and eyebrow as if he was thinking. "I like money. I like cars. I like women. I like nice things. And taking advantage of the fools stupid enough to get caught up in gambling on sports sure has made me a rich guy."

"What are you going to do with us?" she demanded.

He shook his head. "Hmm. I don't know yet. I'm not so sure my normal tactics will work on you guys. I got to think on that a bit."

He shut the door, leaving them in the dark again.

Teagan sat in silence in the pitch-black. Officer Cory, the only one who hadn't been bound by ropes or shot, had removed everyone's tape from their mouths a few minutes prior, but no one spoke. The only sounds heard were the quick breathing from him as he fought to untie Lacey, and also from Mrs. Dodger who'd been untied first and was now working on Ryan's ropes.

"Got it." Cory announced. "You get Teagan. I'll get Betty."

Lacey tugged on the ropes around Teagan's wrist. Quicker than Teagan imagined, her hands were free, and Lacey moved onto Teagan's legs. As soon as the restraints were loosened, Teagan crawled across the ground, feeling her surroundings.

"Aunt Connie, where are you?"

"I'm right here." The sound of her aunt's voice comforted Teagan as she reached her.

Teagan fought to free her aunt's feet then moved on to her hands. The last knot released, and Teagan wrapped her arms around Aunt Connie. Her aunt recoiled and sounded like she sucked air through her clenched teeth, obviously in pain.

Teagan drew back. "I'm sorry."

"No, please. Aunt Connie grabbed Teagan and held on tight. "I'm okay."

Teagan lightly returned the hug.

"We are going to get out of here. Impossible is nothing." A tear fell from Aunt Connie's cheek onto

Teagan's hand.

Teagan nodded. "Yes, impossible is a dare." She clamped her teeth together, insisting that her own tears stay where they were.

Suddenly a moan came from Ryan, finally waking from the beating he'd gotten before Teagan had come upon him at the YASO building.

"It's okay. I'm here. You'll be okay." Mrs. Dodger said. Teagan couldn't see, but she imagined his mom rubbing his head.

"What's going on? Ouch. Ouch. Oh." Ryan moaned.

"I'm sorry," his mom said. "I know you are injured pretty badly. These ropes are so tight. I'm trying to be careful."

"Where are we?" Ryan asked.

Mrs. Dodger explained everything that had transpired.

"I'm sorry, Mom. I'm so sorry. This is all my fault. I should have gone to Teagan's dad as soon I started receiving threats."

"You were only trying to help. I know. I should have done the same thing and gone to Officer Wright when I realized what my brother was mixed up in."

"How did he get involved in it?" Aunt Connie asked.

"My brother, Max, was a good man. He started YASO, but he wasn't perfect. After attending a horse race at Churchill Downs with one of our athlete mentors, Terry Timbers, two years ago, he introduced Max to a high-end, exclusive, and illegal, underground sports gambling ring out of Louisville. Soon, the ring found its way into the Knobs and dug its claws into several of its wealthy citizens. Max got so caught up in it that he started taking money from YASO to pay back his gambling debts. Max had felt such guilt over all of it that he finally told me. He made me promise I would take it to my grave. After his death, I started receiving threats that if I didn't pay back what Max owed then they were going to hurt me and Ryan. Max owed them well over fifty-five thousand dollars. I drained my bank account and gave them every penny I could scrounge, but they wanted the rest of the twenty-one thousand. I didn't know what I was going to do, but I refused to take from YASO or gamble myself. I took every extra client and odd job I could get. But that didn't even put a dent in what was still owed."

Teagan had to know. "Ryan, how did you get mixed up in it too?"

"About a month ago . . ." Ryan struggled to get his words out as he breathed heavily, "down at Romeo Court in New Albany, some Hispanic guy told me about my uncle's debt. He threatened he'd hurt my mom if I didn't get it to them by the end of the month." Ryan's voice shook as he spoke.

A chill ran down Teagan's neck and arms. Now she understood. He'd done it all for his mom. He was the same, good guy she'd always known. "Was the guy's name Pedro?"

Ryan nodded. "Yeah, I think he works for Marco."

"He does." Betty confirmed.

"I had no clue how to get cash like that, and I didn't want to scare my mom." Ryan continued. "The next day at Romeo Court, Teagan's crazy neighbor's nephew, Julian . . . Do you remember him?"

"I do. He's who put us in here," Teagan told him.

Ryan scoffed. "It doesn't surprise me. The dude

was cool the first night I met him. He bet me he could beat me. He lost, of course, and I made twenty bucks. Then he told me about how I could make real money, but it was a high-class, fancy event and I needed a suit and tie and some skin in the game to start betting. He loaned me $2,000 and took me to my first sports gambling event. Some local government officials and big names in sports were there. We had to sign some agreement that we wouldn't reveal names, et cetera. I thought it was awesome. I was going to make some money and network for my future basketball career. I had no idea it was illegal. It all seemed legit. I mean, horse betting is okay over at Churchill Downs. The gambling boats are down on the river, and even the Indy 500 has betting tents set up now. I'm eighteen so I thought why not try to earn some easy cash. I won five hundred dollars that night. Then a thousand the next and twenty-five hundred the next. I paid the dude back the $2,000 and I used my earnings to keep betting. I thought if my luck continued, I'd have the money in no time."

He sounded like he seethed in pain between his teeth, but he continued. "After a total of three weeks,

I'd earned just fifteen hundred shy of what Uncle Max owed them. I was hoping Pedro would let the small amount slide, since I was a kid, but Julian showed up instead. When he found out I didn't have the full amount, he told me he would break my shooting arm if I didn't get the other fifteen hundred to him by the next day. I thought it was no problem, I'd earned more than that several times. I went one more time to the sports betting club, but this time, I lost twelve hundred dollars. I was then twenty-seven hundred short. Julian told me he would only forgive the debt if I threw my game the next night. They had a lot of big names looking for a sure win. I knew high school betting was illegal, and if anyone found out I threw a game I would lose my scholarship. I refused and told him I was going to the cops, and that I was done gambling."

"Good for you," Aunt Connie said.

"He let me know he had cops in his pockets and that I was in for life now. I could never get out. He had footage of me gambling, and he would leak it if I didn't do everything he told me to. If I didn't listen, I was afraid that I'd lose my scholarship and opportunity to play for Indiana University. That's been my dream forever. I didn't know what to do. That's when I told Ty about it. I didn't throw the game the next night and Julian warned I better watch my back because I wasn't safe."

Detective Evans cleared his throat. "That's how they get you. First, it's the prestige and the easy cash that draws you in, but then the losses start coming, and you realize no one's your friend unless you're winning." He drew in a deep breath. "And then more losses keep coming, and your bank account is empty in no time . . . and your wife is asking where all the money has gone. And then threats start coming, and they tell you everything you worked your whole life for is going to be destroyed if you don't pay or do exactly what they tell you. I worked my whole career to make detective."

"Who's talking?" Ryan asked.

"Detective Chase Evans with the Floyd County Sheriff's Office. I'm who Julian thinks he had in the back of his pocket, but not anymore. I'm done with him."

"Yeah." Lacey said, "Well, you're basically dead if we don't find a way out of here."

"We will." Aunt Connie sure was a determined

woman even when everything seemed stacked against them.

Ryan asked, "I know why Julian's after me and the detective, but why you guys?"

"I don't know." Teagan answered.

"He knew we weren't going to let it rest until we figured out who hit Ty." Confidence rang in Aunt Connie's voice again. "His stories were starting to not add up. Teagan and I would have figured it out in a matter of hours, I bet."

Teagan didn't know about that, but yes, something had seemed off about Julian, and she would have started seeing through him soon enough. She was sure of it. She wasn't some naïve girl blinded by good looks and charm. He had fooled her a little, though. That was stupid of her.

She hated being stupid.

Voices and footsteps could be heard upstairs.

"Shh." Aunt Connie touched Teagan's hand.

Was that Dad's voice?

Teagan strained to hear but couldn't make out anything they were saying. Surely, he was looking for her and Aunt Connie.

"Should we scream?" Teagan asked. "I think

that's my dad."

"What if it isn't and we make them mad?" her aunt questioned. "Or what if it is, and they've captured him too. Who will be looking for us then?"

She was right. Screaming wouldn't have any benefit either way.

Aunt Connie continued, "We have to figure out how to escape."

"It's impossible." Mrs. Dodger interjected.

Teagan sat up. "Impossible is not a fact. It's an opinion. Impossible is not a declaration. It's a dare. Impossible is potential. Impossible is temporary. Impossible is nothing."

"Oorah." Aunt Connie let out a quiet battle cry.

"Oorah." Ryan echoed.

"That's motivational, but we need a plan." Lacey said.

"The only option is to be a team," Detective Evans suggested.

Did he even know how to be a teammate? Teagan rather doubted it. "How?"

"We will have to fight back together," the detective said.

"And how do you presume we do that." The

aggravation spilled from Lacey's tone. "You can't even stand. Most of us are injured, and does anyone besides the crooked cop in the room even know how to defend ourselves against Julian?"

"I do." Aunt Connie still held strong to her confidence. "Teagan's dad taught me how to protect myself from enemies. Just like I'm sure he's trained you, Teagan."

"Yes, he did."

"And Ryan and I were trained in self-defense by Mitchell Brink." Mrs. Dodger interrupted.

"The celebrity fitness trainer?" Lacey asked.

"Yeah."

"I took a course a few months back, but I know very little." Lacey gave a scared laugh. "The Dodger family really does know everyone. Mitchell Brinks. That's amazing."

"It was because of my brother. He had unbelievable connections. Too bad Terry got him mixed up in all this. But I can't blame Terry. Max is responsible for his own action."

Aunt Connie cleared her throat. "And sounds like in the end Max was trying to get back on track."

"He was. He really was."

"Nice sentiment here, but let's get *back on track*," Detective Evans grunted.

Teagan nodded, but in the dark, no one could've seen her. If only that was her dad upstairs and he knew they were down here. Would the police realize that Betty was missing, and then search her bakery, apartment, and basement? She had called 9-1-1 and said they'd found Ryan at YASO, but then no one would have been there. Surely, people were out looking for Betty now too. And if Dad had tried to call Teagan or Aunt Connie and they hadn't answered then he would have looked at his phone to track Teagan's whereabouts. He'd surely have gone to find her wherever her phone was and realized she and Aunt Connie were missing too. Where was her phone and glasses? Had Julian destroyed them? Maybe Dad hadn't been able to track the phone's whereabouts. Maybe he thought their phones were just dead.

A scared tear threatened to fall again, but she refused to let it. They were going to get out of here. Dad would find her. He knew Aunt Connie and Teagan would never let their phone even get close to low battery.

The voices stopped and then a door slammed.

Silence.

If that had been Dad, he was gone now.

Please, someone find them before Julian returned.

Chapter Thirteen

Home Court Advantage

The sound of footsteps coming down the stairs startled Teagan. Please be someone who'd come looking for Betty. But if not and it was Julian, she prayed everyone was ready to fight for their lives.

The door slid open, and Julian stepped inside holding a lantern in one hand and a gun in the other.

Teagan's heart raced as she surveyed the room. Everyone, except Officer Cory and Detective Evans who hadn't been tied up in ropes, pretended to still be confined by them. Officer Cory sat huddled in the corner, arms across his knees as if restrained by his own fear. It was all a part of the plan. Detective Evans was the only one not having to pretend. He remained unable to move in a pool of blood under and beside his shot leg. His face looked pale, but somehow, he was still fully conscious. Ryan and his mom leaned against the wall, head-to-head.

Aunt Connie sat a few feet away, alone, with dried blood caked on her forehead, down her temple to her cheek. Most of her hair had fallen out of her bun. Her red dress shirt ripped at the collar and untucked from her black dress pants. Her feet without shoes. Where were her aunt's heels? Probably with Teagan's glasses.

Aunt Connie would hate seeing herself like this.

Lacey lay on the ground beside Teagan. The injuries to Lacey were worse than Teagan had seen in the faint light from the flashlights. Deep gashes, bruises, bloody ripped clothes, and swollen eyes. She must have put up a good fight.

Teagan clutched her fist. Whatever it took, she would get all of them out of here, and Julian would pay, even if it meant sacrificing her own life. He wouldn't hurt another person. She'd be sure of it.

"Are you guys ready to play ball?" Julian's gruff tone no longer held any trace of the kind boy she thought she'd met. "I'm here to strike a deal."

"Never," Teagan shouted.

He bent down and ran his hand holding the gun along her cheek. "Such a shame. I really kind of sort of liked you, but if you guys aren't willing to play then I must dispose of you."

"Is that supposed to scare me?" Teagan hoped she sounded braver than she felt.

"In your case, I am going to have your dog killed and make you watch." He let out a villainous laugh. "Does that scare you?"

"You took my dog?" Teagan glared at him. He wouldn't get the chance to hurt Colonel Mustard.

"Yeah, he's been such a good little fellow, but his bark is insistent. Good thing the place I put him is fairly soundproof."

It took every bit of willpower to keep from attacking him.

He paced the room. "I could have put you all there too, but what would be the fun be in that? Here I can frame Betty for your murders. Since she hides dead bodies in her basement and all. But then again, I could starve Colonel Mustard and then I could feed you all to the dogs, literally."

"What is your problem, Julian?" Ryan didn't sound afraid of Julian either. He'd always been the kind to stand up to a bully. "Why are you doing all of this?"

"I needed leverage for when Nancy Drew and her sidekick, here . . ." Julian waved his gun in Teagan's direction. ". . . finally solved this mystery. It's been quite a fun game veering Teagan off track. I especially liked the part where Colonel Mustard became my best little buddy. Too bad I'll have to put him down."

Who cared if Julian knew she was no longer restrained in ropes? Forget the plan. She lunged at him. With one hand against her chest, he pushed her flat onto her back. Pain immediately shot through her head, and she wasn't certain, but she thought she was bleeding.

No one spoke or moved. Her head throbbed. She wasn't sure if it was bleeding from hitting the ground or if she was sweating.

Julian circled the room as he pointed his gun at each of them. "Who is going to go first?"

Teagan's heart raced. They weren't going to make it out alive. She'd ruined the plan.

He stopped at Betty. "Well, you'll go last of course because after you freaked out when you caught all these people in your basement spying on you with cops and detectives, you realized you had no other choice and you killed everyone, then yourself."

Betty shook her head. "No one would believe that."

"But they already do, don't they?" Julian smirked. "You said you catch people down here all the time."

"Why would she shoot Teagan?" Aunt Connie asked. "She's like a mother to Teagan."

"When our secrets are revealed, aren't we willing to do anything to keep them that way?" He stood over Teagan and pointed the gun down at her. "I do what I have to do to keep the status quo."

"Leave her alone," Ryan shouted.

Julian leaned down into Ryan's face. "Sorry, what was that? Did you say something?" He put the gun to Ryan's forehead. "Shut up, or you're first."

Aunt Connie questioned, "And what story are you going to weave as to why we would all be down here?"

"Nancy Drew and her Hardy Boys were looking into Ty's hit and run of course, and Teagan needed one more look at that green pen."

Teagan looked at Betty for a reaction, but her eyes held confusion.

"Betty, let me get you up to speed. You stole Teagan's green pen. The most recent one she's been using from the set that her mom gave her. You know the green with the gold one she uses all the time."

Betty shook her head. "I didn't take any pen."

"Of course, you know about the pen. Who in this town hasn't seen her with these special pens? I planted the green one on your desk that day you caught Teagan and me in your basement. I wanted her to think you were the one trying to frame her."

"Why would you want me to think it was Betty?"

He shrugged. "Why not. It was a part of the game. Takes any suspicion off me. I lucked into Teagan being blamed for Ty's hit and run, and that you were my uncle's next-door neighbor. You were an easy pawn in my game. Strike up a friendship, see what you knew, and plant evidence that continued to point in your direction." He pointed the gun at her.

"Does you uncle know what you've been up

to?" Aunt Connie asked.

Julian scoffed. "Yeah, right. Uncle Charles is clueless. He talks a big game and listens to those police scanners night and day, but he had no idea what I was doing right under his nose until he saw that video footage. Now he's lying with the dogs."

"You killed your uncle?" Teagan touched the back of her wet, sticky head. Definitely blood.

A devious look spread across Julian's face. "I told you I like to instill fear not kill unless I'm left without a choice. No, my uncle, like you, is thinking about whether he wants to join me or leave me an orphaned boy twice. My dog Killer is making sure Uncle Charles and Colonel Mustard behave."

"You are insane." Ryan blurted.

"I like to say mentally unstable. Sounds more like something my therapist would say. Blame it on the untimely death of my parents and my upbringing by my uncaring, selfish uncle." He turned and pointed the gun at Ryan. "Speaking of dumb uncles, yours was the wussiest man I've ever met. He was literally scared to death like a little girl. Died from a heart attack when he had a gun held to his head."

Ryan lunged at Julian, knocking both of them

onto the ground. Teagan and the rest of them jumped to their feet, ready to defend themselves. Her head pounded, but she had to forget about that now. Julian pushed Ryan off him and shot him in the front of his left shoulder. Ryan grabbed his arm and collapsed to the ground. His mother ran to him.

"Leave him." Julian yelled as he pointed his gun at Mrs. Dodger.

"Despite what you think you can't control me. You're going to kill me anyway, right." She put her arms around Ryan and held him against her.

"Fine. Have your two minutes."

Julian turned toward Lacey and Teagan. Teagan stepped forward. Fists ready. Adrenaline pumping. Maybe Julian was a sharpshooter, but Teagan couldn't just roll over and give up. Ryan stood and his mother followed along with Aunt Connie. They surrounded him in a semicircle like a pack of dogs about to attack their prey.

Julian laughed and pointed the gun at each of them. "Just a bunch of—"

A low growl came from behind him.

Colonel Mustard edged his way towards Julian, completing their circle. Where had he come from?

Relief washed over Teagan. Her dog had found her. Maybe they were going to be okay after all.

Julian looked toward the door. "How did you get here?"

While Julian wasn't looking, Teagan grabbed his gun with both hands. She twisted it to the right, breaking his finger, forcing him to drop the gun. Thank goodness Dad had taught her that move.

Lacey grabbed the gun and pointed it at Julian.

Good move, Lacey.

He laughed. "Like you are really going to shoot me." He jutted his head forward, challenging her, but she backed up. "Like I said you aren't going to shoot me."

"I'm ready to take you down, though." Ryan held his fist in front of him.

"Me too." Teagan swept Julian's feet out from under him, and he smacked his head on the ground. "Doesn't feel good, does it?"

Colonel Mustard hovered over Julian. The German shepherd snarled and barred his teeth.

"Easy, Colonel." Julian should pay for all he'd done, but that didn't mean Teagan wanted her dog to hurt him.

Jail time. That's what Julian deserved. Locked up like a caged animal.

Aunt Connie grabbed a rope and tied Julian's hands above his head while Colonel continued to guard above him.

Lacey moved in closer with the gun. "I'm not afraid. I'm just a better human being than you. But I will shoot you if I have to."

Julian jerked, trying to break free of the ropes.

Aunt Connie looked down at herself and tucked in her shirt, and then pulled her hair out of the bun. She smoothed it and returned it to a bun. "I've got to find a way to keep my hair in place. This mystery solving is wreaking havoc on my wardrobe." She winked at Teagan then gave her award-winning smile.

Footsteps thumped on the stairs. Teagan clutched her fist, prepared to fight again if she had to. Mr. Lewis, a bleeding gash on his forehead, stood in the doorway with Killer. Colonel Mustard lifted his head then pointed his snout downward at Julian.

Mr. Lewis shouted up the steps "They're down here."

More footsteps.

Dad swung passed Mr. Lewis and went to Teagan. He threw his crutches on the ground and put his arms around her and then he held his arms out for Aunt Connie. She fell into them.

After holding her father and aunt tight for a good minute, Teagan let go and looked up. Gary stood in the doorway with Mr. Lewis. "How did you all know we were here?"

"We didn't." Dad admitted. "Mr. Lewis found you."

"Actually, it was Colonel Mustard," Mr. Lewis said. "I knew my nephew had to be up to no good. I haven't seen him for years and all of a sudden he just ups and moves here. Acting like he's takin' care of me in my old age. He thinks I'm an invalid, but I'm as fit as a horse. I just don't like being around people much is all."

That was an understatement.

Mr. Lewis cleared his throat. "Anyway, I thought I'd do a little detective work myself after I found that video of the Mustang peeling out of the YASO parking lot. Such a shame what happened to your friend." Mr. Lewis gave one nod to Teagan.

Had he actually said something kind? She

raised the corners of her mouth in a slight smile.

He continued, "I swore the fuzzy image of the driver was Julian, but I wasn't positive until I found your German Shepherd locked up in the cellar behind my old body shop down at The Point. No one else knows about that storm shelter. One summer in a tornado when he was a young boy, we hid out there."

"You mean you left me out there in the dark all alone for hours." Julian wiggled, again trying to break free from his constraints.

Colonel Mustard remained hovering over Julian.

"Stop being dramatic," Mr. Lewis barked. "It was only an hour or so. I was checking to see if there was any damage to my shop and vehicles."

"That's the only thing you ever cared about." Julian fought against the ropes.

"I'm ashamed of you. Hitting me upside the head with a shovel and locking me up in that cellar with the dogs. Too bad your dog likes me better than you. Killer and that police dog busted us out." Mr. Lewis told Julian.

Teagan glanced at her shepherd. "Good boy."

"I taught you the difference between right and wrong, didn't I?" Mr. Lewis put his hands on his hips. "How to earn a respectful income. Not off the backs of others. I worked my tail off my whole life to provide for you after your parents died. Did you learn anything from me?"

Julian turned his head away from his uncle. "Only how to be a mean piece of work."

Mr. Lewis crossed his arms over his chest and turned. He looked over his shoulder at Teagan's dad and gave a head nod then patted the side of Killer. "Come on, boy."

The Pitbull followed Mr. Lewis out the door and up the steps.

Gary stepped into the room. "I need to take Julian in. Colonel, stand down."

Colonel Mustard drew back and sat next to Teagan wagging his tail as she petted him. Gary pulled his handcuffs from his duty belt.

"Wait." Aunt Connie stated as she put her foot on Julian's chest. "I want to make an accusation. The crime was committed by Julian Lewis in the YASO parking lot with a yellow Mustang." She pretended to drop a microphone. "And that's how a

Nancy Drew wannabe solves a case."

Dad smiled. "This is one game of Clue I'm glad you won and it's finally over."

Chapter Fourteen

The Ball is in His Court

Teagan and Aunt Connie entered Mr. Lewis's yard, but he didn't yell at them to leave. Instead, he invited them onto the porch. Killer greeted them at the top of the steps and rubbed his head against Teagan's side.

"Hey, boy. You doing good?" She patted Killer then held her hand out to Mr. Lewis. "Thank you for finding us."

He nodded. "With the help of Colonel Mustard. He wouldn't relent until I followed him there." Mr. Lewis rubbed his forehead. "I'm sorry for everything my nephew put you through. I blame myself and bad parenting."

Aunt Connie leaned forward. "You took that

boy in when his parents died. I'm sure you did your best."

"I could have done better."

"You could be better and be there for him now." Aunt Connie touched his hand. "Paul says with all they have on Pedro and Julian, it sounds like Julian, at least, will be in for life. Maybe your affection will soften his heart and change him."

Mr. Lewis put his other hand on top of hers. "Thank you for saying that, but it's impossible. The damage is done."

Teagan and Aunt Connie looked at each other. "Impossible is a dare."

Chapter Fifteen

The Sixth Woman

Teagan sat a few rows behind the players on the bench at the first Indiana University Basketball game of the season. Dad on one side of her and Aunt Connie, who'd come in town to join them, sat on her other side. Lacey and Mrs. Dodger sat with them also.

The announcer called the name of the starting forwards then the center. Teagan clapped.

"Next starting at guard, freshman Ryan Dodger."

Teagan screamed and clapped.

Dad turned and looked at the people around them. "That's her boyfriend."

"Dad." Teagan gave him wide eyes.

"What? I'm proud of him. He had a lot to come back from."

She looked at the scar on Ryan's arm from the bullet wound. Yes, he had.

The announcer called again. "And the other starting guard, freshman Tyrese Jones."

Dad pointed to Lacey. "And that's her boyfriend." Then he pointed to Teagan again. "And her best friend."

Teagan made big eyes. Lacey reached across Aunt Connie to squeeze Teagan's hand. Who would have thought a year ago that Teagan and her arch nemesis would be college roommates at UChicago, let alone incredibly good friends again?

Ty tossed Teagan the peace sign as he ran out onto the court. Ryan threw his arm over Ty's shoulder.

She stood to her feet and cheered. Months of physical therapy and healing, but Ty and Ryan had risen above what was meant to destroy them. Julian hadn't won. By the end of the half, the scores were very close, but IU was ahead by a couple of baskets. The teams jogged off the court, but Ty and Ryan sat on the bench and glanced toward Teagan.

Yep, this was going to be fun.

Lacey leaned toward her. "Did you tell your aunt yet?"

"Tell me what?" Aunt Connie grinned.

"It's a surprise." Teagan shook her head.

"I don't like surprises."

"I told them you didn't." Paul pointed to Teagan and Lacey then toward the basketball court as if pointing toward Ty and Ryan who were no longer on the court.

Lacey touched Aunt Connie's shoulder. "You will like this one. I promise."

Aunt Connie smirked. "We'll see."

A man cleared his throat beside Aunt Connie. "Excuse me," he said. "You're Connie Wright, correct, with the Wright Foundation?"

"Yes, I—" Aunt Connie turned and looked up at the nearly six-and-a-half-foot brown complected man. Her jaw dropped. "Are you Roland Langley from the Brooklyn Bouncers?"

"Yes, ma'am. Your niece Teagan heard I was coming to watch Ty and Ryan play tonight and asked if I'd come introduce myself because you are a big fan."

Aunt Connie cheeks turned about as red as her heels. Was her aunt actually blushing?

"I am a huge fan. Your behind-the-back, reverse 360 dunk is my favorite."

"Yeah, it's my favorite too. I'm getting ready to perform at half time. Want to come out with me? I've got the perfect dunk to include you in?"

"No way." Aunt Connie's face lit up. "I would love to."

He took her hand and led her down the arena steps to the sidelines next to the scorekeeper table as the announcer said, "Tonight, let's welcome Brooklyn Bouncer, Roland Langley to the court for some half time entertainment."

He waved and ran on to the court as someone threw him a ball. Aunt Connie stayed at her spot on the sideline. Roland did several trick shots and slam dunks while the Brooklyn Bouncers theme song played. The crowd roared with each basket.

Finally, he motioned for Aunt Connie to join him. Wearing a cordless mic, his voice could be heard over the speakers as he introduced her to the crowd. He then had her stand a few feet from the basketball goal.

He walked backward while dribbling the ball toward the sideline. "You ready?"

She nodded and smiled from ear to ear. "Should I take off my heels?"

"No, ma'am. The more height the better. Just stay right there." He dribbled the ball toward her then threw it hard against the court. The ball bounced high in the air as he leapt upward with sprawled legs over Aunt Connie while catching the ball. He slammed it into the goal and landed on his feet next to her. She jumped up and down, clapping her hands and cheering for him. He held the ball under his arm and gave her a double high five.

"Now, it's your turn." He tossed her the ball. "I'm going to teach you some moves."

He taught her how to spin the ball on one finger, how to pass the ball to him off the elbow and she repeated these moves successfully several times.

"Go, Aunt Connie." Teagan cheered for her aunt.

"Now. Let's do that 360 slam dunk you love." Roland handed her the ball.

"Me? That's impossible."

"Impossible? I heard you don't believe in

impossible."

"True. Impossible is a dare."

"I dare you to trust me."

She raised her eyebrows and nodded. He ran behind the scorekeeper table and returned with a mini trampoline. He placed it in the same spot he'd had her stand when he'd done the slam dunk over her. "Now, would be a good time to remove those heels."

She slid them off and threw them to the side. The crowd cheered.

"Your aunt is the coolest," Lacey said.

Teagan agreed. "Without a doubt I want to be just like her someday."

Lacey nudged her. "You are pretty close already."

"Stand on the trampoline toward the goal and hold the ball." Roland told Aunt Connie. "Be ready. When you are in the air in front of the basket, slam it into the goal. I've got you, don't worry."

Roland backed toward the half court line. "You ready."

With her back to him, she nodded. "Yes."

"Here I come!" He darted towards her, then

jumped onto the trampoline and wrapped his arms around her waist simultaneously as he bounced them into the air and spun them 360 degrees. As soon as the rotation was complete, Aunt Connie slammed the ball into the basket and the crowd went wild. Roland safely landed them on the ground.

She turned and threw her arms around him. "That was amazing."

He returned the hug and two more sets of arms wrapped around her. She looked at them. Ryan and Ty.

She looked at Ty. "I can't thank you two and Teagan enough for making this happen."

"It was our pleasure." Ryan and Ty said in unison.

The crowd continued to cheer.

"Greet your fans." Ryan suggested.

She pulled away from the group hug and pointed toward Teagan, Dad, and Lacey then looked back to Roland. "If you ever need another player, hit me up."

"I know the Brooklyn Bouncers would love for the Wright Foundation to help organize our next charity event game. And I most definitely want you to play with us. You game?" He raised an eyebrow.

"That's one game I can't wait to play."

Aunt Connie posed for pictures with Roland, and she received several high fives and handshakes on her way back to her seat.

As soon as she sat, the teams returned to the gym and ran to the court for the start of the second half. Ty swayed back and forth, his feet planted in place, waiting for the ball to be thrown in. Ryan, on the adjacent side, blocked out his opponent. Teagan's heart raced. She'd missed watching them play. Being at different schools and several hours apart, she wasn't able to make many games in person, but she watched what she could on TV.

The official handed the ball to the opposing player out of bounds. He threw it in. Sneakers squeaked against the court as the players moved for the ball.

The lights went out and everything went dark.

The sound of the basketball landing on the floor echoed across Assembly Hall.

A female screamed and cell phone flashlights lit the gym. One of the players from the other team was missing from the circle, and a cheerleader yelled,

"Where's Tina? Oh, my goodness, where's Tina!"

Dad darted down the bleachers. Off to help. No surprise there. The sound of people speculating spread through the gym.

Aunt Connie looked at Teagan and raised her eyebrow. "Up for solving another mystery?"

Teagan smiled. "Sure, Nancy Drew."

The Assembly Hall lights flickered back on. "Excuse me, everyone." The announcer came over the loudspeaker. "No reason for alarm. Edwards and Tina have been found safe and sound."

Aunt Connie snapped her finger and winked. "Until next time."

The Visitor Kids Around

Preview by Dena Netherton

Skye Wright jerked awake at the crash of breaking glass and a child's high-pitched shriek of terror. She jumped out of bed and threw on her robe. Was one of the children hurt? What had broken? Her heart pounded at the thought of one of her foster care children being injured.

She threw the bedroom door open. "What happened? Is everyone okay?"

Silence met her ears. She sucked in a deep breath and dashed down the hallway.

Samuel Fortier, her business partner and property caretaker, met her at the top of the stairs. He looked as disoriented as she felt. Could he have heard the crash from his cottage behind the foster care mansion? She cinched the sash on her robe tighter. "Sam?"

"I decided to check the doors to make sure they all had been bolted before heading to bed. Sounds like it came from one of the south rooms." His characteristic unruffled bass tone hid any emotion even though he raked his disheveled black hair away from his face.

Skye followed him down the hall, but before they could discover which room the crash had come from, a little girl bounded out of the Sea-Star bedroom sobbing then flung herself on Skye.

"What is it, Athena? Are you hurt?" Skye held the little girl, stroking her hair.

"My window! It broke, And now it's all over my bed." She looked over her shoulder as if fearing the shards of glass might follow her out into the hallway.

Samuel hurried inside to check the damage.

"I don't wanna go back there. Please, Miss Skye, can I stay with you tonight?" Athena buried her face in Skye's robe, her little body trembling as she continued to cry.

The door next to Sea-Star opened and nine-year-old Rocky stomped into the hall. "Sounds like some terrorists are after Athena." He folded his skinny arms across his chest and made a disgusted face. "Those guys are cowards, going after a little girl."

Athena cried even harder at the boy's words.

"Man, if they want to mess with someone, they should deal with me." The boy thrust out his chest and narrowed his eyes.

Sam stepped between Rocky and Athena, still huddled against Skye's waist. "Rocky, you should go back to bed. We've got it all under control."

Skye greatly appreciated his assistance. He knew how to handle the little boys and they never gave him any lip.

"Okay." Rocky slumped his shoulders. "But if ya need me, I got my lightsaber under my pillow."

"That's good to know, Rocky. Now, get some sleep." Samuel steered the little boy back into his bedroom.

Skye pressed Athena to her side. "Shhh, it's okay, Athena. You're safe. There aren't any bad guys out there, and no one's going to hurt you. Mr. Sam will make sure of that."

Sam returned, holding his cell phone. He nodded toward Skye's bedroom at the other end of the long hallway. "Put Athena in your room and when she's settled down, meet me downstairs. I've already called the police. They should be here soon."

Shawna Robison Young

Enjoy The Visitor's Next Trip

Scan QR code for a direct link for purchase.

From the Story

Karleen's Bits O' Brickle Cookies

Ingredients

1 cup of Bits O' Brickle (6 oz. package)
1 ½ tablespoon of liquid shortening
6 tablespoons of flour
½ cup of butter
6 tablespoons of sugar
6 packed tablespoons of brown sugar
½ teaspoons of vanilla
1 egg
½ teaspoon of salt
½ teaspoon of baking soda
And 1 ¼ cup plus 2 tablespoons of flour

Directions

1. Preheat oven to 325°.

2. In a small bowl mix Bits O' Brickle with liquid shortening until evenly coated, then stir in 6 tablespoons of flour until well coated; set aside.

3. In a large bowl, combine butter, sugar, brown sugar, and vanilla; beat until creamy.

4. Beat in egg. Gradually add salt, baking soda, and flour; mix well.

5. Stir in coated Bits O' Brickle.

6. Drop rounded teaspoon onto greased cookie sheets.

7. Bake for 10 to 12 minutes.

8. Makes fifty 2 - inch cookies.

Wrong Way Out by Lill Kohler

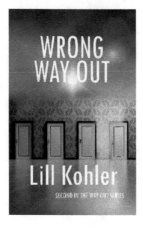

When There's Nowhere to Turn

What would you do if your world suddenly changed overnight?

Lucy Grossen lost it all, but Nathan Burrows came to her rescue, much to the displeasure of Walker Stewart. Nathan challenges Lucy and Walker in several ways to think beyond what they see. When they follow Nathan's leadings their lives are changed forever. Then life takes yet another twist and Lucy and Walker are plunged into another adventure.

Malcolm Greenfield isn't sure he can trust Marla McCluney, but out of his loyalty to a deceased friend he sticks around to help her. When Marla's life seems to be threatened Malcolm seeks the help of Lucy and Walker.

Will they help? Will they offer hope to a couple they don't know? And how far will they go to help?

When things look bleak there is always hope that someone will come along and help you get your feet back on the ground.

Shawna Robison Young

Acknowledgments

I am excited to be given the opportunity to join the Write Integrity Press team for the Visitor series. Thank you to Betty Thomas Owens for suggesting me for this project. Also, thank you to Marji Laine for including me with this group of great authors.

Thank you to my husband, kids, and parents who are my number one fans and listen to me talk about my imaginary characters and their lives for hours on end.

Thank you, readers, for taking the time to read this story. It means the world to have your support. If you enjoyed the book, please share it with others.

Heavenly Bits O' Brickle cookies included in the book was inspired by my grandmother's recipe. She baked them every Christmas for our family. I hope you like them as much as we do.

About the Author

Shawna Robison Young loves all things chocolate especially a warm cup of hot chocolate and sea salt caramel truffles—daily requirements for her busy life. Being the mother of three teenagers and one elementary age child, she's normally on the go from one sports game to the next then on to a theatre or dance performance, church camp, and more. She cherishes the time she and her husband of nearly twenty- five years served together as worship and children's ministers.

Writing and teaching are Shawna's passion. Whether it's singing the ABCs with students at the preschool she owns, sharing what she's learned with new writers, or passing along Bible truths to her children ministry classes, she's a teacher at heart. Her dream vacation spot is Hawaii. Maybe one day she'll make it there. If so, she will be found lying on the beach enjoying the sun on her face or playing in the waves with her family.

Connect with Shawna Robison Young at
https://www.shawnarobisonyoung.com/,

on Facebook at
https://www.facebook.com/shawnarobisonyoungauthor/,

or Instagram at
https://www.instagram.com/shawnarobisonyoung/

Letter to Reader

Dear Reader,

> *Impossible is not a fact.*
> *It's an opinion.*
> *Impossible is not a declaration.*
> *It's a dare.*
> *Impossible is potential.*
> *Impossible is temporary.*
> *Impossible is nothing.*
> *-Muhammad Ali*

I use the Muhammad Ali quote a few times in *The Visitor Plays a Game.* His statement reminds me that when life and challenges seem impossible that is when we should laugh in its face and keep fighting. Turn to God. Impossible is nothing with Him on your side. Know who you are and whose you are. Trust God has a plan and a purpose in all your impossible situations.

Also By Shawna
The Unsuspecting Heather Meyers

What if you've returned home to start your life over, only to discover you're there to finish it?

Ready for a fresh start, Heather Meyers flees from not-so-sunny California to her hometown in Indiana. But fate has other plans—stage IV cancer and three months to live.

Determined that one more kick from life won't destroy her faith, Heather fights against its schemes. Before she can take her final rest, redemption must be found for someone she loves.

Physical therapist Dr. Jack Jones (JJ) would do anything to change the past, to not have let his high school sweetheart get away. Now that Heather's back, he'd do anything to keep her from leaving. With her time running out, he may never get his chance to set things right.

By a twist of fate and with an extra dab of this and a little bit of that, nurse Anna Ingram sets out to prove that JJ is more than his past mistakes and Heather can find hope and love in the midst of the biggest battle of her life.

Thank you
for reading our books!

Please consider leaving a review for the author
on the purchase page for this book.

Look for other books
published by

P

Pursued Books
an imprint of

W

Write Integrity Press
www.WriteIntegrity.com

9 781951 602192